Professor Diggins

John

Jarmes

Orson

Mary
Abby

Lydia

WEEKLY READER CHILDREN'S BOOK CLUB
presents

Professor Diggins' Dragons

by Felice Holman

illustrated by Ib Ohlsson

THE MACMILLAN COMPANY,
NEW YORK
COLLIER-MACMILLAN LIMITED,
LONDON
This edition is published by arrangement
with the Macmillan Company

For everyone, young or old,
who has ever had a crock of butter
to carry around a mountain . . .
and met a dragon.

Library of Congress catalog card number: 66-16103
The Macmillan Company, New York
Collier-Macmillan Canada, Ltd., Toronto, Ontario
Printed in the United States of America

Weekly Reader Children's Book Club Edition
Intermediate Division

Contents

CHAPTER I

Tea, Cakes, and a Rumor

At first the decision to retire Professor Diggins from the University looked like a real disaster. The idea was just not going to be popular. It was not going to be popular with Professor Diggins, who preferred teaching to doing anything else. It would not be popular with Mrs. Diggins who, though she dearly loved and admired the Professor, preferred to kiss him good-bye in the morning and know that he was happy and busy with his classes of students at the University, to having him lope about the house all day, looking for things that could not be found.

But most of all the idea was not going to be popular with the children who lived near Professor Diggins' house on Guardian Hill, because it was part of their daily life to walk with the Professor on their way to school, and on *his* way to the University, and at that time to hear stories and riddles and songs and ideas about all manner of things that were exciting enough to carry them through spelling and arithmetic and well into civics.

"What goes on and on," Professor Diggins had asked suddenly one day, "on and on, never slacking, never stopping, never leaning, never dropping, never reaching, never bending, never turning, never ending?"

"What?" young Orson Peale, Jr., asked eagerly.

"Good heavens!" the Professor had exclaimed. "That *is* something to think about! I shall get right to work on it. Hmmm. I once knew a man," he continued, with hardly a breath between thoughts, "who was only four feet high. He was the biggest man I ever knew."

"Biggest!" cried Jarmes McGill. "Four feet tall! I'm taller than that myself."

"Ahhh!" said Professor Diggins. "You're talking about 'tall' and I'm talking about 'big.' We will pass each other in the dark that way." And so on, right up to the school gate every school day of the year.

Well, and finally, the idea to suspend Professor Diggins was not going to be popular at the University itself, where nearly everybody would miss the Professor's presence, except possibly the janitor of the biology building, who would find his work much easier without buckets of sand all over the floor, all kinds of broken sea shells, wet globs of seaweed, sticky jellyfish, squashed beach plums, not to mention the distinctive aroma of fish too

long out of the sea—all left after Professor Diggins'
famous classes in marine biology.

And yet, in certain respects, Professor Diggins was a
very orderly person, particularly around his head. His
hair was gleaming white, parted right down the center
and laid to each side in equal neat fringes. His collar,
rather too high and stiff to be stylish, was always immaculate because it was celluloid and all he had to do to keep
it clean was run it under the faucet each morning. Mrs.
Diggins kept his black coat brushed and tidy for him, and
his waistcoat, which fitted snugly, was hung with a great,
gold, beautifully polished watch chain. However, there
was no watch on it.

But the farther one got from Professor Diggins' head,
the less orderly he became, and that may have been because he was unusually tall. By the time he got to his
feet, it would seem he had lost interest in dressing entirely. They were always unpredictably attired—in house
slippers, in mismatched socks, in tall laced boots from his
days in the infantry, and, on occasion, completely bare,
because he sometimes just forgot to dress them.

Still, it was not his unusual appearance which had anything to do with the University's decision to give him a
kind of rest. On the contrary, everyone at the University
was devoted to Professor Diggins' appearance. It was not
that at all. It was a rumor.

Rumors are nasty things and the directors of universities are always having to disregard them—strange or unpleasant things that people say that they have heard other people say about somebody else. The University directors had been disregarding rumors about Professor Diggins for quite a while. He was, after all, one of the country's most outstanding authorities on marine biology. They simply could not afford to listen to rumors about so rare a person. They did not even pay much attention when the rumor reached them that Professor Diggins had been seen on the beach counting grains of sand. He had, as a matter of fact, been able to explain it to some extent.

"It occurred to me," Professor Diggins had said at the time, "that it is possible that there are more grains of sand than units of anything else in the entire world. Each grain of sand, after all, was once part of something much larger. A great many secrets and much history is in the sand."

"But were you *counting* the grains?" the Administrator asked.

"Ah, well, that's only a beginning, of course," Professor Diggins had said at the time. And, at the time, when the Administrator had repeated the conversation to the Chancellor, it was considered that it was not a matter that was going to be improved by further questions. And they had let it drop.

There were other things, of course; but the thing that finally got them worried was the rumor about the dragons. At first they let it go, nervously, but then, when the complaints started coming in from the parents of several students, it seemed something had to be done. The Chancellor, as usual, gave the job of questioning to the Administrator, who, as usual, had no choice.

"Professor," the Administrator asked kindly, "is it true you are lecturing your classes about dragons?"

"Oh, yes," said Professor Diggins in an offhand way, as if the matter were in no way unusual. And then he started wandering about the Administrator's study, reading the titles of books on the shelves. "Oh, yes."

The Administrator was put off his stride, because he had planned his questions expecting the Professor to say, "Oh, no." Professor Diggins climbed the library ladder to examine the books on the topmost shelves, taking a few out of their places and powdering everything below with dust. A spider, who had been living quite undisturbed between *Applied Periodicity* and *A Study of Pyrodynamics* was forced to look around for a new home. The Administrator coughed and frowned at Professor Diggins but kept to the matter at hand.

"By dragons," the Administrator began, suddenly seeing a gleam of hope, "I wonder if perhaps you could have been discussing dragons as an imaginary form of sea life?"

Professor Diggins considered this, leaning back from the ladder precariously. "Generally the matter of sea monsters is optical and most often delusional," he said. "No, I was referring strictly to the conventional, fire-breathing, earthbound dragon. A regular dragon."

"A *regular* dragon!" whispered the Administrator. "I see."

"These books probably keep your study very warm," said the Professor, picking up *A History of Labyrinths,* thereby displacing the spider for the second time.

"Now, Professor, I hesitate even to ask such a question of you, but I have been told—and I suppose it is just one of these cases of lack of perfect communication—but I have been told that you are suggesting that dragon hunting be revived as a sport," and the Administrator made an attempt at a laugh, which was a total failure.

"Oh goodness, no," Professor Diggins said.

"Well, thank heaven!" exclaimed the Administrator, and he leaped to his feet and reached across his desk to shake the Professor's hand.

"Not as a sport," Professor Diggins continued, "but as a serious and considered pursuit."

When the Administrator came back to make his report the Chancellor was throwing darts tipped with suction cups at a dart board on his door. He did this whenever he was nervous. "Are you quite certain?" he now asked the Administrator.

"No question about it," said the Administrator miserably. "But really, in all other ways he seems quite all right."

"All other ways!" exclaimed the Chancellor. "When a man is organizing the students to go dragon hunting, the other ways in which he is all right are not important." And he threw another dart.

"I don't know that he is *organizing* them," said the Administrator doubtfully. "He just *suggests* it, that's all."

"That's all!" The Chancellor peered closely at the Administrator, and the Administrator blushed. "What, exactly, did he say? I'll have to have it in the report to the Trustees."

"Well, he just said that a great many useful things were out of style and people are the worse for it."

"Yes, yes! But about the dragons?"

"Well, he said years ago dragon hunting was quite usual. If people thought there were dragons around, they put on their armor and went out and hunted them . . . no second thoughts about it. They didn't let them just keep roaming about scaring everyone. Now, he says, we just pretend there are no dragons."

"Pretend!"

"That's what he said."

"All right," the Chancellor sighed. "That's that!" And he aimed another dart.

"Are you sure there's no other way but to retire him?" asked the Administrator.

"My dear Administrator," said the Chancellor, "even in normal times a university has responsibilities. But these are not normal times. At this moment I am trying to get one million dollars from rich old Davenport Pym to help this university over a very difficult financial crisis and to build a new gymnasium. Now, I ask you this. If *you* were Pym and had a million dollars to spend building a gymnasium and making your name important in the traditions of a university, would you put it into a school that was supporting dragon hunting? Or would you cast around for a school with a good basketball team. Ha? What do you say to that?"

But in the end, even the Chancellor could not bring himself to retire Professor Diggins. Anticipating all the people the idea would not be popular with, he decided to let the Professor finish out the spring term and then persuade him to take a fine long vacation instead of teaching in the summer session. As to the fall term, they thought then perhaps they could extend the vacation or if necessary keep him busy doing research or *something*. But sufficient unto the day. Much to their relief, Professor Diggins said he thought a summer vacation would fit in with his plans very well.

When the people on Guardian Hill learned that the Professor would not be teaching at the summer school, nearly every parent's mind turned in the same direction.

"If only," said Mrs. Murdo McGill, "we could persuade him to hold some summer classes for the children. My Lydia and Jarmes enjoy his company so much."

"Just what I was thinking," said Mrs. Orson Peale, Sr. "Little Orson thinks the world of the Professor. They are both intellectuals, and," she said, lowering her voice, "it would get Orson out from underfoot those awful long summer days."

"Why not ask him?" said Mrs. McGill. "What could we possibly lose?"

Mrs. McGill invited Professor and Mrs. Diggins to tea. She served small sandwiches made to look like layers of ribbons, iced petits fours, and two kinds of tea, China and India. Lydia and Jarmes McGill sat quietly under the hall table, out of sight of their mother, but in view of the tea table, whose delectable display they nervously watched disappear.

"He's got a fearful appetite," hissed Jarmes to Lydia.

"Especially for ribbon sandwiches," mourned Lydia.

"He's eaten thirteen petits fours," said Jarmes.

"You're not supposed to count, you know," Lydia said.

"I forgot," said Jarmes.

Mrs. McGill addressed herself to Professor Diggins. "We hear," she said delicately, "that you will be free this summer."

Professor Diggins smiled. "I am always free, madam—as, I trust, are you. The question is to what use we put our freedom."

Mrs. McGill turned a very pretty pink which exactly matched one of the iced cakes.

Mrs. Diggins said kindly, "I believe Mrs. McGill was speaking of your vacation, Prosper."

"Ah, yes," Professor Diggins agreed. "Ah, yes."

"Several of us have been wondering," Mrs. McGill resumed, "if you would consider—just *consider*—taking some small classes of children during the summer. They really do think so much of you, you know. Your stories fascinate them and . . . " Mrs. McGill was getting quite carried away with herself.

Beneath the hall table, Lydia jumped so suddenly that the vase on top of the table bobbled and would have fallen if Jarmes had not reached out and caught it brilliantly. "Did you hear that?" whispered Lydia. "Classes! With the Professor!"

"Fourteen petits fours," said Jarmes.

"Ah, would that I could," the Professor said kindly. "Would that I could, but I can't. As a matter of fact, I shan't be on Guardian Hill this summer. I shall be off."

"Off where?" inquired Mrs. McGill. "If I may ask?"

"Indeed you may," replied the Professor. "I am off on a small hunting expedition along the coast."

"Prosper has got a little old bus and he's put a cot in it," said Mrs. Diggins. "I've made the curtains myself. It's quite neat."

"Expedition for what?" asked Mrs. McGill.

Since Professor Diggins' mouth was now full of ribbon sandwiches, Mrs. Diggins answered for him. "Part of his work is collecting marine specimens for study, you see. Since he will have more leisure this summer he thought he would camp out in a pine grove on the coast for a few weeks and that way be able to study the shore more closely."

"Might get in a bit of dragon hunting, too," Professor Diggins said into his teacup. Mrs. McGill gave a rather nervous smile and took a sip of tea herself.

"I suppose," said Professor Diggins, suddenly looking up from his cup, "I could always use a few assistants. Yes," he went on after a moment or two of thought, "it might be an idea at that."

"Take the children along, do you mean?" asked Mrs. McGill, very wide-eyed. "I'm not sure . . ."

"Couldn't take many, of course," said the Professor. "Couldn't get many more cots in the bus. On the other hand . . . " And the Professor gazed off into space, quite ignoring Mrs. McGill who was talking.

"Off? For weeks! In a bus! Well, I don't know . . ."

Under the hall table, Jarmes clamped his hand hard

over Lydia's mouth to keep her from giving a whoop. For himself, he was grinning so widely he looked like a Halloween pumpkin, his teeth being spaced rather that way.

"I'll think it out," Professor Diggins was saying as he rose. "And now we really must go. Thank you for the beautiful tea."

Professor and Mrs. Diggins stood in the hallway putting on their coats. Lydia and Jarmes could have reached out to touch their legs. Suddenly the feet of Professor Diggins backed up until Lydia thought they would step right on her. Then two enormous hands appeared below the table right in front of the children's faces. In each hand were two ribbon sandwiches and a petit four. Lydia looked at Jarmes, her eyes wide in a question. Jarmes looked back and shrugged. Then the fingers on the hands wiggled meaningfully, calling attention to themselves. Lydia nodded to Jarmes and they both reached out and took the food. Then the hands waved ever so slightly and disappeared. The legs moved away. The door closed.

CHAPTER II

A Trip to the Sea

Professor Diggins never wasted time. He did not spend hours pondering details. He simply made up his mind and then went straight ahead. Thus, having made up his mind to take the children along, it became only a question of how many more cots could fit into the old bus. The answer was five, if they didn't take much luggage. "One change of clothes each," said Professor Diggins, "and a toothbrush."

Mrs. Diggins was doubtful. "The girls should have something pretty for dress-up," she had said. "in case they want to look especially nice, and swimming suits and—"

Professor Diggins cut her off firmly, but he agreed to the swimming suits. He waved away the dress-up clothes with a flick of his long fingers.

Mrs. Diggins had been working on the bus for several weeks in advance, beginning when the Professor had first

announced his intention of making the trip alone. She
had done wonders. All along the outside of the bus was
a row of window boxes planted with vegetables—carrots,
parsley, radishes, peas, beans, lettuce, peppers, and a box
of petunias just for gaiety and decoration. A trellis rose
from the boxes of peas and beans, and they were climb-
ing rapidly under her daily supervision and care.

Although the plan was to cook out of doors most of the
time, Mrs. Diggins had made a rainy-day kitchen in the
front of the bus, with a little spirit stove on top of the
icebox. She had fitted a small cupboard with cups and
dishes, silverware and linens. "You may wish to rough

it," she said, "but sometime you may tire of that and wish to use some nice china and silver." So she put in a set of her good Meissen, packing it carefully, and some handsome silverware and a good damask cloth.

She had curtained the windows of the bus with blue and white checked gingham, and when it was decided to take the children, she had cut the big curtain to draw across the center of the bus to make a girls' dormitory and a boys' dormitory. She remembered to hang a mirror on the girls' side. All in all, it was bright, efficient, and homey.

And so it was on a Monday morning in July that a great many people were standing in front of Professor Diggins' house saying good-bye—that is, a few were standing. Others were hopping, jumping, waving, skipping, calling, and hugging. And then Professor Diggins kissed Mrs. Diggins good-bye and held the door of the bus open for his five companions. They were

Lydia McGill, eight. Completely at home in the world. Dainty, vivacious, warm, and well-liked by all despite . . . oh, well, never mind about *that* right now.

Jarmes McGill, ten. A good brother to Lydia,

though a tease sometimes. Energetic, enthusiastic, and forgetful.

Orson Peale, Jr., seven. Round-eyed, round-mouthed, round-bodied. Bright enough to be much older than he was.

Mary Abby Byrd, eleven. Big and capable, but a bit shy and unsure. Mrs. Diggins told her privately that she was counting on her to look after the smaller children and see that they washed now and then and drank their milk.

John Pascal, nearly twelve. Tall, manly, a great reader and just on the verge of being a great writer and a great many other things.

All the other children from Guardian Hill were there to see them off, wishing, oh, wishing so hard to go too, but they were too young.

And then the bus was off, leaving Mrs. McGill still breathless, Mrs. Diggins happily waving her handkerchief, Mrs. Peale sighing with relief, and Mrs. Byrd and Mrs. Pascal shedding a tear or two.

The Professor drove the bus down the main highway and out to the open country, humming a tuneless kind of tune and occasionally fitting in such words as occurred to him on the spur of the moment.

Straight ahead to the traffic light
Go two miles and turn to the right
De da dum—diddle dee dee
Instead of two miles make it three.

And eventually, following his own directions, he got completely lost. But it didn't seem to trouble him a bit.

Lydia and Jarmes played tic tac toe for the first half-hour and then found that they were missing too much scenery, so they spent the next hour window watching.

There was surprisingly little conversation. They sat looking out of the window, watching things of moderate interest with moderate interest but thinking a lot.

Mary Abby felt a pang about leaving home. She was worried about her kitten, too. Her mother had said she would feed him and not to worry, but Mary Abby worried anyway.

John was thinking he hadn't brought nearly enough books to last for the whole trip, but the Professor had said there just wasn't any more room.

Jarmes had a nagging feeling for just a minute or two that his mother had asked him most particularly to do something and he had forgotten what it was. It didn't bother him long.

Orson was restless. He couldn't wait to get to the ocean and really start the vacation.

Lydia was completely relaxed. She rested her head against the back of the seat and said, "You know what's nice, I think?"

"What?" asked John.

"Riding along and no one trying to make us play games, like counting cars from out of the state, or red trucks, or barns with hexes."

"Or trying to find animals in the clouds," said Orson.

"Or adding the numbers on the license plates," said Jarmes. "That is really awful."

"What I really hate," said Mary Abby, "is people trying to cheer me up when I feel car sick. If I feel car sick, I shall be car sick and I would rather be car sick without the cheering up."

The Professor had another ditty going now, this one in

a minor key. The meter was a bit unsteady and there was no refrain. It just went on . . . partly like this.

> *Turn to the right*
> *The sea's in sight.*
> *Turn to the west*
> *That might be best.*
> *Turn to the east*
> *I like that least.*
> *I'll go straight ahead*
> *Instead.*

It really did seem, if you listened, that he had no plan for the trip at all and was just turning the bus this way or that as the mood took him. However, it was just about the middle of the afternoon when they turned down a lane shaded by tall pines and came to a stop in a lovely grove on the shore of the ocean.

"Ah, splendid!" said Professor Diggins. "Just as I left it."

CHAPTER III

Settling In

Professor Diggins stopped the bus under a large old pine tree, opened the door, and climbed down to the ground. Then he did a deep knee bend, a few runs up and down in place, and took several very deep breaths.

"Now," he said, "the first thing we have to do is get down there on the beach and take a long look at that splendid shore line."

"But what about setting up camp? What about making the beds? What about fixing the supper and all that?" worried Mary Abby.

"First things first," said the Professor and started off with long strong strides over the pine needles and onto the dunes.

"Goodness," said Mary Abby, "he's not very organized, is he? We'll have to look after him." And then she joined the others who had jumped down onto the pine needles. They stretched their cramped legs and then quickly ran to catch up with the Professor, who had nearly reached the shore.

And there it was! There. There. There. Forever and forever out to the horizon and, as they all knew, even on beyond it. Quiet now, with little low-tide waves licking at their shoes, the shore breeze bringing seaside sounds to their ears. And the miles and miles of shore, sandy, duney, wispy with coarse green grasses, bayberry, beach plums, scrubby pines. Peopleless. Peopleless except for themselves.

Jarmes was the only one of them who could find a word appropriate to the feeling they were all feeling, and what he said was, "Wow!"

For a while, hypnotized, the children wandered along the beach getting the feel of it. Then one by one they returned to the bus and started to busy themselves. And, amazingly, things seemed to get done. Orson helped Professor Diggins set down some of the window boxes outside the bus door. Mary Abby thought there should be a little marked path to the doorway of the bus, so she collected stones of an even size and laid out a very neat walk. Everyone admired it a great deal.

Professor Diggins explained to them about the old well

down the path and about the privy that used to belong to a house on the point, and then John and Jarmes went with a bucket and drew water, and Mary Abby took a broom and swept out the privy. Lydia came back from a walk on the beach with six enormous clam shells to use for bread and butter plates, and then she watched John and Orson set up a picnic spot with four fallen logs around a big flat rock. Mary Abby put up a clothesline and Jarmes made her some clothespins out of razor clam shells.

And then it seemed to be suppertime. Mrs. Diggins had packed them some nice meat patties for their first supper and Professor Diggins grilled them over a lovely fire. They threw in some potatoes and roasted them until the outsides were black, but the insides were white and fluffy. Orson pulled a few carrots from the window box and they munched them happily in the firelight. The tiny icebox of the bus yielded plenty of cold milk and they each drank a large mugful with a nibble of bitter chocolate.

"Now is the time, I suppose," said Professor Diggins, "if we are to do the orderly thing, to make plans, plot our course, delegate chores, and draw up a sort of overall campaign. Right?"

"Right," said Mary Abby, looking encouraged.

"Oh," said Professor Diggins. "Oh, well, if you like

that sort of thing . . ." And he wrinkled his forehead for a moment. Then he brightened. "But, of course, there is the other way—just letting things happen, seeing what tempts us, doing what needs doing as it needs to be done, drifting along . . ." He looked a bit dreamy.

"Oh!" cried Lydia. "Could we do *that?*"

"Absolutely!" said the Professor. "Any objections? Good, that's settled."

"Now," he said. "As to socks."

"Socks?" they all said in unison.

"Yes, socks. The very last thing Mrs. McGill said was 'Remember about their socks.' Does anyone know what she meant?"

"Wear them," suggested Lydia, while Jarmes said, "Wash them," and Mary Abby said, "Change them."

"I was wondering," mused the Professor, "if we might solve the whole thing by collecting all the socks, folding them neatly, and putting them on the shelf of the bus until the vacation is over?"

"Shoes too, maybe?" said Jarmes.

"Excellent!" said the Professor. *"Now* we are getting somewhere."

The air was cool but the fire was warm, and after several minutes of silence, Jarmes said, "Lydia's asleep."

"So's Orson," said John, looking closely at Orson who, at first glance, seemed to be only deep in thought.

"I must confess that the sea air has made me a bit sleepy myself," said Professor Diggins. "If no one has any objections, I think I shall prepare for bed."

Everyone agreed that bed sounded surprisingly attractive. Lydia awoke at a light prod from Jarmes and made a somewhat stumbling journey to the bus. Orson, however, seemed to be asleep for the night, so John and Professor Diggins carried him to his bunk and covered him with a quilt.

No one had the least trouble falling asleep.

CHAPTER IV

A Bedtime Story

In the morning the hot cocoa, cooked up in a big pot and served with a soup ladle, tasted better than hot cocoa had ever tasted before. The Professor made fried eggs on a large flat rock, which he had heated in the fire. They flipped the eggs onto bread toasted over the coals, and Orson said that it might possibly be the best breakfast ever.

"What will we do," worried Mary Abby, "when we have eaten all the food that is in the little icebox?"

"Ah, nothing to it," said the Professor. "Every morning, at about this time, a very obliging huckster comes down the main road, and if one of us is waiting there at the end of the lane, he will stop his truck and sell us anything we need."

"Well, we don't need vegetables," said Orson, who had taken a great interest in the window boxes. "I'm glad to see that Mrs. Diggins planted so many carrots. They're a remedy for night blindness, and I particularly want to see well at night."

"Well, we will need more milk and bread right away," said Mary Abby.

"I'll go down and get them," said Orson, and taking up the enormous tin pail for the milk, he started down the lane to meet the huckster.

Mary Abby said she would do the dishes, and Jarmes, feeling very good and energetic after his delicious breakfast, offered to get the water from the well and, furthermore, he promised to see to it that Mary Abby always had water for the washing up. Not to be outdone, John dried the dishes. Lydia went off to see what was to be seen at the water's edge.

When he had returned with the milk and bread, Orson began following Professor Diggins around to see what he was up to. He was up to something quite interesting, it turned out. He was starting to work on the salt water tank for collecting specimens. It was a large glass and metal container which had been well secured to the back of the bus, just under the petunias.

Professor Diggins started by putting a layer of very small stones in the bottom of the tank. Orson helped and then went to find some more of the same size. Then the Professor put in a layer of charcoal, which he had brought for the purpose of keeping the water pure. The charcoal was covered by larger stones and then considerable sand.

"Now," said the Professor, puffing a bit from the effort, "we are going to need buckets and buckets of sea water. Any ideas?"

"Mmmm," said Orson. "How about a bucket brigade?"

"You mean," said the Professor, "passing a bucket of water along a line of people, all the way up from the shore? But there aren't enough of us to reach."

"Leave it to me," said Orson, and he raced around the grove and down to the beach, gathering everyone together.

A few moments later, when the Professor looked up from the tank, he was surprised by a most energetic scene. The children had formed a line perpendicular to the shore. Orson dipped the bucket full of sea water and passed it to John, John passed it to Mary Abby, Mary Abby passed it to Jarmes, Jarmes passed it to Lydia, by which time Orson had run around to the top of the line and accepted the pail from Lydia, and John had run up next to Orson, and Mary Abby had run up next to John, and so on. They kept passing the bucket and running to

the top of the line over and over again until they reached the Professor.

"Upon my soul!" said the Professor. "That is the most ingenious method of carrying a bucket of water I have ever encountered. Now all I need is about another ten bucketfuls."

Getting ten buckets of water up from the sea by means of Orson's bucket brigade might not have been easier than carrying them up one by one, but it was more exciting. By the time the tenth bucket was dumped into the tank, however, Professor Diggins said he thought they might postpone until the next day starting to collect specimens for the tank.

Everyone agreed that a swim sounded better, and they spent the rest of the afternoon ducking under the breakers and lying on the sand.

Supper was enormous bowls of rich beef soup, a window-box vegetable salad, and some of·the fresh bread Orson had gotten from the huckster that morning. When Mary Abby started to do up the dishes after supper, she discovered the water bucket was empty. Jarmes struck his forehead with his palm, "Ooooo, I forgot," he moaned, and grabbed the bucket and ran down the path. Lydia laughed. "See if he *ever* remembers," she said.

Day had turned into evening so softly and so perfectly that no one noticed it happen. The sea had moved way down the beach, the sun set somewhere behind the pine trees, the gulls disappeared from overhead, the sky darkened. The wind blew cool from the water and they moved closer to the evening fire. The pines stood around them dark but friendly. Guarding.

Orson said, "Professor, wouldn't tonight be a good night to tell us one of your stories?"

And as everyone seemed to think that the best possible of ideas and said "Please" very nicely, Professor Diggins said, "Why, yes, I think this is a very good time for a story." And after another moment he said, "I think I shall tell you a story about dragon hunting."

"In olden days," (Oh, marvelous! the children thought. Good stories often began that way) "in, say, England, a country wife might say to her country husband, 'Here is a crock of freshly churned butter. Carry it around the hill to my old mother, and hurry home before dark.'

"So the good country husband, willing or not, would take up the crock of butter, tuck it under his arm, trudge out across the field, and begin to climb the hill. Then, as dusk began to fall, the shadows cool and lengthen, and the wind began to rise and cry, a dragon might suddenly appear around the turn of the hill . . . breathing fire, possibly.

"Well, now, *there* was a pretty good reason to turn back. So running into the town, calling 'Dragon! Dragon!' the country husband would rouse the citizens and tell them of the terrifying creature that had obstructed his progress around the hill. Then, the next day, they would all be up at dawn, and getting out shields and lances, swords and bludgeons, and a goodly supply of pots and pans to beat on, they would all go out and hunt the dragon together. And somehow, sharing his fears with the others, the country husband got braver, and he brightly led the whole party out onto the hillside and showed them the place where he had seen the dragon."

"And did they catch it?" asked Lydia.

"Well . . . catch it?" considered the Professor. "I don't have the actual statistics, of course, but the thing was to frighten it away, at least. Keep it from blocking the path around the mountain, you see. At the very least, the country husband had some mighty fine company going around the hill and back."

"He would have been a lot braver if he had gone after the dragon himself, " said John.

"Only perhaps," said the Professor, "because sometimes it takes more courage to admit fear. And then, of course, some dragons were extremely large and took more fighting than others, and people were always glad to help. Anyhow, that's the way it used to be."

"Is that the end of the story?" asked Lydia.

"Yes and no," said the Professor. "Really it goes on and on. I can tell it another way. Let us suppose that the man, humming a little tune and clutching the crock of butter, rounded the turn of the hill, saw the dragon, took a quick look, then turned on his heels and ran back down the mountain. Then let us say he sneaked quietly home, threw the butter into the well, and told his wife he had a fine trip . . . pretended he was never afraid, you see, and that there was no dragon at all.

"Now, the next time she asked him to take some butter to her old mother, the dragon would have grown a bit. And the next time bigger, and bigger."

"And all that butter going down the well," said Jarmes.

"And the old mother . . ." wondered Mary Abby, ever practical. "Wouldn't she say, 'Where's the butter you said you were going to send me?' "

"Ah, yes," sighed the Professor, "those would be some of the complications. And then after a while we have this big, strong countryman who goes through his entire life unable to carry a crock of butter around the hill."

"Is *that* the end?" asked Lydia.

"For the time being," said the Professor, and he got up and wandered down to the shore.

"The Professor's stories are so peculiar," said Mary Abby. "They begin all right, but then something happens and everyone doesn't just live happily ever after."

"The Professor once told me," said John, "that some of the best stories don't have an end. They just come to a stopping place. We get used to hearing stories in books that finish up once and for all. Things don't usually happen like that."

And then everyone seemed to think it might be bed-time. And it did look pleasant—each cot made up with crisp white sheets and folded blankets, smelling faintly but beautifully of camphor.

Professor Diggins returned from his walk along the shore, and while the children were settling in and falling asleep he busied himself making some notes about the beach and tides in a little red notebook. When he thought everyone was well established, he switched off his battery lantern and was just putting on a rather handsome sort of skating cap and preparing to climb into his cot when he heard a sound like a cat meowing. Professor Diggins was not a professor for no reason at all, and it did not take him long to discover that it was not a cat, but that the sound was coming from the bunk occupied by Orson.

"Hmmm," said Professor Diggins to himself, and went back to see what was to be done.

"Ahoy, young Orson," said the Professor in a soft voice. "What seems to be amiss here?"

At first Orson only continued to make the catlike sounds, but eventually he snuffled and said, "I'm trying not to cry. The others would laugh at me."

"Ah, you're doing quite well at it," said Professor Diggins. "I would never have thought you were crying myself. It sounded most misleading. You can take comfort in the fact you will never be found out." Orson looked entirely pleased for a moment and stopped making the catlike sounds.

"What sort of thing was the cause of it?" asked the Professor, sitting down on the edge of Orson's cot.

"The truth is . . ." Orson began.

"Oh, yes, for heaven's sake, only bother with the truth," said Professor Diggins. "We don't want to waste time with anything else."

"Well, then," said Orson, "I'm an intellectual person,

you know, and even though I recognize this is a wholly emotional and perhaps irrational thing, the truth is I'm afraid of the dark."

"Ah," said Professor Diggins.

"At home," said Orson, "I leave a light on in the closet."

"I see," said Professor Diggins. "And we have no closet." And he thought about the matter for a moment. "The light," he said finally, "is so you can see what is all around you. Right?" Orson nodded, snuffling a bit.

"You see," Professor Diggins went on, "in the daytime all the spaces around us are filled with familiar things . . . things we recognize. At night we can fill those spaces with things of our imagination and sometimes we fill them with things from the dark side of our imagination."

He shone his flashlight around the bus. "You see," he said, "in the light there is nothing but cots and sleeping children. Now, when I turn off the light you may fill all the spaces in between with things you choose. Why not choose some pleasant things?"

"Like what?" asked Orson, extremely interested.

"What do you like?" asked the Professor.

"Jellybeans," said Orson.

"Well, if you insist," said the Professor. "You could try it. Fill in all the spaces with jellybeans. Pack it solid. Then you might try eating your way out. Let me know

how you make out in the morning." He stood up and gave Orson a pat on the head, and then turned toward the front of the bus.

"Okay," said Orson enthusiastically. "Okay. Thanks a lot. Thanks a lot."

"Of course," Professor Diggins said, turning back, "that's only a beginning."

"What do you mean?" asked Orson.

"Well, you are not going to want to sleep surrounded by jellybeans forever, you know."

"No," agreed Orson, "that's true. But I could switch to candy corn, or marshmallows . . . everything!"

"Or *nothing!*" said Professor Diggins. "You see, it goes

a bit further than you think at first. The night may come when even divinity fudge may not appeal, when you may grow to dislike or dread entirely this forest of confection you have built around yourself. Therefore, I would suggest that you start with jellybeans, switch to candy corn, in moderation, and taper off on marshmallows. When you have seen that you may fill the night spaces with anything you like, it will occur to you that there was nothing there in the first place to frighten you. Then you are free to let the spaces stand empty, tranquil, and quiet."

"I'm starting right now," said Orson, and he squeezed his eyes tightly shut and started piling jellybeans around Jarmes' cot. By the time he had them up to the level of the pillow he was fast asleep.

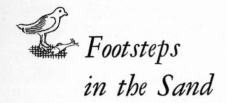 *Footsteps
in the Sand*

John awoke early with the strong feeling that the day was so perfect that not a minute of it could be wasted, and he walked along the shore before the others had opened their eyes to the morning.

The tide was way up the beach, but John could tell it had been even higher a while before because the sand was still wet. Gulls and terns screeched and dived into the curling waves, and sandpipers ran back and forth at the water's edge as though attached to the waves by strings. John stared at the horizon, and the sensation that he was standing right at the edge of the world was so real that he became dizzy and sat down. He twirled his fingers in the sand and started to draw a picture. It turned out to be a seagull. He drew another and couldn't help admiring it. He thought perhaps he might be a rather good artist someday. He drew another and then crawled a bit further along the sand, drawing one seagull after another. It was when he drew his twelfth gull that he saw the first footstep. And then another, and another.

That's strange, he thought, standing up. They come out of the sea, but where do they go in? And he started to follow the footsteps, which seemed to be made by large rubber boots. They crossed the wet sand, their heavy soles making a distinctive crisscross pattern, then became blurry in the dry sand and then disappeared entirely into the beach grass and brush.

John turned and followed the footsteps back to where they began at the shore. A gull screamed over his head and swooped to the beach, and then another two gulls. They stood so close to John's drawings that the drawings seemed to be shadows of the real gulls. John turned back. He hoped everyone was up. He was getting hungry. He picked up some driftwood for the fire as he crossed the beach and arrived at the little picnic grove just as Professor Diggins was lighting some kindling.

"Good morning, Professor," said John.

"Good morning, my boy," said the Professor. "You've been for a walk at the very best possible time . . . when the world of the sea and the world of the land seem more than ever to stand edge to edge—two different worlds."

John looked surprised. "That was just the kind of feeling I had," he said.

And then everyone else arrived from washing and dressing and said "Good morning" and Orson asked, "Where have you been, John?"

"Oh, just walking around near the water."

The air was cool and the children had put on warm sweaters without anyone telling them to. Professor Diggins had made hot milk with a great deal of sugar and a little vanilla. Lydia said "Ugh!" quietly to Jarmes before she tasted it, and then she said, "Oh, this is delicious!" and drank two mugfuls.

"It's a funny thing," John said, "but *someone* has been on the beach this morning."

"You," said Mary Abby, sensibly; "you just said you were."

"Besides me," John said.

"We haven't seen anyone on this beach since we've been here," said Jarmes, "except, of course, us."

"Well, this is a lonely stretch of beach," Professor Diggins said, dipping a donut into his hot milk, "but it isn't our very own. Everyone can come here if they can find the road. They don't bother much, though. Nothing here, you know—no popcorn stands, games of chance—just beach, sky, birds, and water, water, water."

"What makes you think someone was on the beach?" Orson asked John.

"Footsteps," said John. "Great big footsteps, coming

up out of the ocean and crossing the sand, into the scrub."

"Ohhh!" Lydia cried. "Maybe it's a dragon!"

"There's always that possibility," said the Professor, "but identification is most important. Mustn't go hunting dragons that aren't there, just as we must hunt them if they are."

"It's a human being," John said. "Did you ever hear of a dragon wearing boots . . . great big boots with criss-cross patterns at the bottom of them?"

"Nothing to prevent it," said the Professor. "But it's not a clue either way."

"But if it's a man," asked Orson, thinking deeply, "how did he come up out of the ocean with boots on?"

No one had any answer for that.

Later in the afternoon the Professor started a leisurely walk down the beach: looking in the air, looking out to sea, standing still and seeming to look at his feet, stooping and picking up something and putting it in his pocket, putting something else in a little bucket he carried, muttering, bending and digging a little hole in the sand, sifting sand through his fingers, taking out his little red notebook and scribbling something. . . .

It started with just Orson trailing along behind the

Professor. Now and then he saw something that intrigued him and bent to look at it and, if it was really as interesting as it seemed, picked it up and put it in his pocket or in a little tin can he carried. Then Mary Abby, Jarmes, and John joined the walk, and even Lydia, who had been lying in the sun, got interested in what was going on. Before long they were all stooping and picking up whatever struck their fancy, discarding some of it, putting bits of this and that in rolled-up skirts, or clutching things in their hands—twisted ropes of green, brown, and rosy seaweed, cushions of Irish moss, prickly sea urchins, sand worms, little crabs, clams and oysters, tiny fish, snails and mussels and shells, shells, shells. Jarmes

specialized in starfish, which were plentiful on the rocks in the cove.

And when the sun was getting well into the west, Professor Diggins turned back and walked briskly along the tide line, humming, and the children, a bit weary and rosy from the sun, yet somehow refreshed, followed quietly.

Back at the bus, Professor Diggins said he would use all the seaweed that had been picked up, and he laid it or floated it in the salt water tank. Then he put in some periwinkles he had collected, and Orson offered his sand crabs, which went straight down and burrowed into the sand at the bottom of the tank. John had some fine sand worms and Mary Abby had several perfect soft-shell clams. Lydia had found a razor clam. "A beauty!" the Professor said, and Lydia was pleased.

When Professor Diggins told Jarmes he could put his starfish into the tank if he liked, Jarmes slapped himself all over, looked in his pockets, and then said, "Ooop! I think I forgot and left them on that big rock at the end of the cove. I'll go and get them."

Everyone watched with interest as the creatures settled into the tank. The crabs made themselves quite at home and the snails started cleaning house immediately.

But when Jarmes came puffing back from his race to the cove he had something else on his mind. He gave the starfish to Professor Diggins but paid little attention as the Professor thanked him and put them gently into the water.

"Listen!" Jarmes said quite excitedly. "I saw some of those bootprints that John was talking about this morning. Gee, I don't know. They look awfully strange. It could be . . . well, something mysterious!"

"What kind of something mysterious?" asked Lydia nervously.

But Orson cried, "Let's go see! Come on!" So with Jarmes leading the way, the children sped to the shore with the Professor loping along behind.

When they reached the edge of the water, Jarmes ran up and down the beach a way looking closely at the wet sand. "Hey!" he exclaimed. "This is the place, all right, but the prints aren't here."

"Jarmes!" said Lydia sternly. "Did you make it up?"

"No, of course not," Jarmes protested. "Don't be silly. I saw them—great big boot sort of marks with crisscrosses in them, just like John said. *Now* where are they?"

And no one had an answer for that, either.

A New Way with Sheets

Although Professor Diggins had no watch on his gold watch chain, he did have an unusual alarm clock. Early every morning the clatter of clams and oysters dropped by the gulls onto the roof of the bus, as they had their breakfast, was enough to awaken the Professor, though the rest of the sleepers usually only turned over and had another hour's sleep.

So it was one morning that Professor Diggins was up with the gulls as usual, and running in and out of the waves with the sandpipers, collecting jellyfish. Mary Abby, too, had awakened early, dressed quietly, and had gone out to collect tinder for the fire. She lit it, poured fresh water into a saucepan, and by the time the Professor came back from the beach she had cooked a pan of oatmeal.

Professor Diggins was pleased. "It's lovely," he said,

sprinkling on sugar, pouring on milk, and melting a big lump of butter into the cereal. "And smooth," he said, after he had tasted it. "Mary Abby, you are an unusually practical girl for your age, you know."

"I know," said Mary Abby, "because . . ."

The Professor waited, but Mary Abby was quiet. "Because?" he prompted her.

Now Mary Abby blushed, but she said very softly, "Because I'm not pretty." She stirred the oatmeal over the fire quite busily.

Professor Diggins looked up from his bowl. "Aren't you?" he said with surprise, and he peered at her. "I hadn't noticed that, Mary Abby. Are you sure? Where did you get the idea?"

"I just feel it," she said. "A person knows it if she's plain and awkward, and I'm always stumbling over things."

"Perhaps you only think so," said the Professor.

"No," said Mary Abby. I'm just that way, that's all." Oatmeal had never been so well stirred before.

The Professor gave the matter some thought. "Well, of course," he said slowly, "I'm not in touch with the fashion in young girls these days, being a rather oldish man with lots of other things taking my attention, but I have noticed one thing; girls sometimes turn into beauties all in a wink. It would seem as though they just suddenly felt beautiful. And feeling beautiful is, as everyone knows, only a step from being beautiful."

"No," said Mary Abby "not me. I know I shall never have the kind of fun pretty girls do. And that's why I have to be sort of practical, you see."

"Yes," said Professor Diggins, "I see. I see very clearly that right now there is something standing between you and the fun." Mary Abby looked up from the fire.

"And just because you are such a practical girl," the Professor continued, "perhaps one day soon you will see what that 'something' is and just chase it away." The Professor smiled and looked straight into Mary Abby's eyes. "You're not a finished person yet, Mary Abby," he said. "Think about it."

"All right," said Mary Abby. "I'll think about it. Have some more oatmeal, Professor."

And then everyone came into the grove for breakfast, and Mary Abby was busy filling oatmeal dishes . . . each one twice, except three times for Jarmes.

After everyone had had breakfast, Mary Abby said to the Professor, "Just the same, I really do think that it's time to change the sheets."

"Change them?" replied Professor Diggins. "Mmmm. What were you planning to change them to?"

"To fresh sheets, of course," said Mary Abby.

"Now let's see," the Professor mused. "Fresh sheets. Fresh sheets. I don't seem to remember seeing any."

"But what shall we do?" asked Mary Abby, and then she said, "I shall just have to wash them, then."

"Oh, very good," said the Professor appreciatively. "That's very kind of you, Mary Abby." And Mary Abby smiled and blushed.

"But I have no tub," she said. "Nothing nearly large enough. Oh, dear." And her pleasure was spoiled by worry.

"There's a tub," said John, coming up to join them. "Look!" And he pointed to the ocean. "Biggest tub you ever saw!"

"Splendid!" said the Professor.

Mary Abby looked confused.

"Come on, Mary Abby. Come on, all of you!" shouted John. "Sheet-washing day!" And in a few minutes, following John's directions, they were down at the shore, dressed for the water, each carrying a bed sheet. "Now, follow me," shouted John and plunged into the rolling surf, pulling his sheet behind him. When he was up to his waist he started to swirl the sheet around in the water, and in a minute they were all out there with him. Jarmes held his sheet in one hand, dived into the water, swam underwater for a remarkable distance, and came up, sheet in hand. Then he dived again and the sheet

followed him, under water. His progress could be followed by the white shape writhing and floating, dipping
and turning, like a great fish. It looked like such good fun
that John followed him. Orson, who could not swim underwater, folded his sheet into something like wings, and
pushing it ahead of him in the water and using his feet for
power, he glided about the ocean. "I'm a seaplane," he
said. Mary Abby and Lydia dipped and scrubbed in a
more conventional way.

Professor Diggins, dressed in his astounding striped
bathing suit, lay on his back and floated, trailing his
sheet idly behind him.

When the sheets had been washed and washed, the
children came out onto the sand to discuss drying them.
"I know how," cried Lydia. "We do it in dancing class.
Here, we can dry them like this . . . two of us on one
sheet. Mary Abby, you be my partner. Now take hold of
two corners." And she held two corners of her sheet, and

Mary Abby took the other two corners. "Now, we toss the center of the sheet up, holding the corners tight, and run in toward each other." They did, and the sheet rose in the middle forming a beautiful white balloon filled with air, stayed that way a moment, and then collapsed as the air rushed out and the children separated. "Now again," cried Mary Abby. "Now *everybody* try it."

And soon, when they had caught on to the idea, three sheets at a time were ballooning in a marvelous ballet over the sands.

"I shall take off into the air," shouted Orson and tried it, falling to the sand with a thud and pulling his sheet over him. "You've got it all sandy," complained Jarmes.

With the hot sun, the brisk breeze, and the violent waving and ballooning, the sheets were dried, sunned, and neatly folded before lunchtime.

"I can't think why Mama complains about the laundering," said Lydia. "It's really quite a lot of fun."

CHAPTER VII

A Room
with a View

Considering that there were, after all, five variously tempered children in a bus for several weeks, everyone got along splendidly . . . most of the time. But just every once in a while there was a flare-up. The day, for instance, that Orson used Lydia's hair ribbons to tie up the beans. The day John was nicer to Mary Abby than to Lydia. The day Jarmes forgot to get milk from the huckster. The day John was nicer to Lydia than to Mary Abby. The day Lydia shook sand into Mary Abby's bed . . . by mistake. The day Mary Abby burned the oatmeal. The night Orson woke everyone up counting jellybeans out loud. The day Jarmes forgot the butter. The day John tied Mary Abby's apron to the top branches of one of the tall pines. The day Mary Abby hid John's most exciting book to get even. The day Lydia rested on a rock so long, Jarmes rolled her into the water. The day Jarmes forgot the bread.

It was on one such day that John was trying to read,

and everywhere he sat it seemed someone wanted him to move. He had finished two books and was reading his third, but moving about was really very distracting. When he read a book, he wanted to be in the book, be part of the book. If it was exciting he lived the excitement, and it was very upsetting, just when someone was about to be run through in a duel, to have Orson step right across his legs carrying a bucket of water. And just when the small sailing craft was threatened by a typhoon, Mary Abby started to set the table for lunch.

"Gosh!" John said, "this place is crowded. Every now and then I wish I had a room of my own." And he got up and started looking about for another place to sit down.

"Good idea!" said the Professor, who had just come up with a pailful of enormous crabs. "Why don't you look for a spot that suits you and stake out a claim? John's room, it will be, and no one will disturb you."

"Honestly?" said John. "I can just take a piece of the beach for myself?"

"Has anyone any objections?" Professor Diggins asked the rest, who were gathering for lunch.

"Can I have a room for myself, too?" asked Lydia.

"Why not!" said the Professor. "Each of you can. Just help yourselves. Then what do you say we all come back around four for a swim? Jarmes, since you have a watch, will you rouse us all at four?

"Sure!" said Jarmes.

Right after lunch John went to survey the possibilities. After considering the pros and cons of several locations, he picked out a place right at the edge of the pine grove where he got good light but not the bright sun upon his book. He arranged some fallen logs around the area, piled up some pine needles for a sort of couch, and then tried it out. It couldn't have been better. He found a hollow protected by rocks where he could put some note paper, a pencil, and the book he was reading. He stayed there half the afternoon—long enough to find that the hero recovered from his dueling wounds and the typhoon blew itself out before the ship capsized.

Lydia, meanwhile, was looking for a room of her own. She knew what she wanted and she found it. It was a large flat boulder in the full sun. She brushed the sand

off it and took some small stones from the beach to border it. Then she set herself right in the middle of the boulder and lay on her back. A sun porch!

Orson decided on a laboratory. He had a project in mind. He picked out a protected spot surrounded by large rocks—a natural room with a sandy floor. He took a few food cans that had been discarded, lined them up on a rock shelf, and began to plan his project.

Jarmes set up a crafts studio. He had been working on some ideas he thought he could sell for pocket money when he got home. He had already made some very good ashtrays of big clam shells, and now he was working on shell necklaces for ladies.

Mary Abby set up a housekeeping room near the bus. It had been discovered that she was the only one in the party who could sew, and she had quite a lot of mending to do. As soon as she was settled she began to sew a button on John's jacket.

By the middle of the afternoon Lydia thought that that might be enough sun for a while, so she left her sun porch and went to see if anyone wanted to swim. No one was about. She wandered through the pine grove until she came to a brand-new sign. It read JOHN's ROOM. She saw John on his pine couch, staring out across the water —not reading, just staring. Lydia knocked on a tree trunk. "May I come in?" she asked in a whisper.

John turned around and stood up. "Yes. Come in," he said. "Won't you sit down?"

"What are you doing?" asked Lydia, seating herself on the couch.

"I'm working on an idea for my novel," said John, sitting beside her.

"Oh, I didn't know you were writing a story," said Lydia. "How long have you been doing it?"

"Oh, all summer," said John. "Off and on, of course."

"What's it about?" asked Lydia.

"I think it's about a boy," said John.

"What do you mean you *think* it's about a boy?"

"So far it seems to be about a boy."

"You mean as much as you have written?"

"Oh, I haven't written any of it yet."

"Then how can it be a story?"

"Oh, it's a story all right. I just haven't written it on paper. Not enough has happened to put it down yet. But I have a feeling that any time now something will happen and then I'll start to write it."

"Ohhh!" said Lydia. "I didn't know that was how you wrote a story. I think I could write one like that myself."

"Well, go ahead," said John, waving at the sea and indicating that he was willing to share the pool of inspiration that he was dipping into. So Lydia joined him in staring at the horizon.

After a while she said, "I think my story is about a girl."

"What about a girl?" asked John.

"That's as far as I've gotten," said Lydia and returned her gaze to the edge of the sea and the sky.

Professor Diggins, who had been spending the afternoon making many notes in his very full notebook, decided that it might be time for a swim, too, and went out to see how everybody felt about it. The first room he came to was Orson's laboratory. He knocked on the rock nearest him.

"Come in," said Orson. "I've just been observing these snails."

"Marvelous creatures," said the Professor.

"It is my hypothesis," said Orson, "that the snail actually has a potential for enormous speed *if* he would apply himself to the problem."

"You mean," said the Professor with interest, "that you think these snails could move quite fast if they wanted to?"

"Exactly," Orson said. "My problem is to find out how to make them *want* to."

"Hmmm," said the Professor as he turned to go and find Jarmes, "a most interesting idea!"

The Professor found Jarmes draped in necklaces and bracelets of jingle shells strung on reeds.

"Decorative!" exclaimed the Professor in admiration. "You exude the aura of the South Sea Islands! Now, what I am wondering is if it has gotten to be about four o'clock as yet?"

"Ooop!" said Jarmes. "I forgot. I'm sorry, Professor, but I just forgot to call you. It must have slipped my mind."

"Mmmm. That memory of yours interests me," said Professor Diggins.

Jarmes looked rather pleased. "How?" he asked.

"It seems so . . . well . . . slippery," said the Professor. "So very slippery."

Jarmes laughed. "I guess it is," he said.

"Why do you suppose that is?" asked the Professor, holding up a silvery jingle shell and watching the light come through it.

"I don't know," said Jarmes. And then he said, "Well, maybe I *could* remember sometimes if . . . if I wanted to hard enough."

"Ahhh!" said the Professor. "It wouldn't surprise me if

you could." Then he squinted at the sky and said, "Mmmm, looks like rain."

"But, you know . . ." Jarmes started, and then he stopped.

"But?" asked the Professor still looking at the sky.

"But," said Jarmes, thinking hard and looking at the sky, too. "Sometimes it's sort of handy . . . not remembering."

"Just so!" said the Professor, looking pleased and giving Jarmes a pat on the back. "Just so! Mmmm, might not rain after all. There's nearly enough blue in the sky for a Dutchman's breeches. Small Dutchman. Shall we swim?"

CHAPTER VIII

Possibilities

There were a lot of sounds on the beach in the early evening, even though at first one thought there were none—the waves breaking, the gulls screaming, the wind gusting. One evening, on top of these noises, in between them, and woven around them was a kind of high-pitched music that was not familiar to the shore. It sounded like a song in pain.

Professor Diggins looked about in confusion. He knew the seashore so well, but this sound was a bit out of the way. He moved in the direction it seemed to be coming from, and then he saw John in his private room, flute to his lips, blowing and frowning and blowing and frowning and producing something that was as far from music as it was close to it.

Professor Diggins waited for a pause and knocked. John looked around and frowned completely.

"What ho?" said Professor Diggins. "Have we a musician in the party, then?"

"No," said John, "you certainly have not. It's just that I promised my mother I would practice, and now I have a room of my own I thought I could do it without anyone saying how awful it sounds."

"You don't really want to play the flute?" asked Professor Diggins.

"No," said John. "No." And then he erased the frown and sighed, shaking his head in a resigned fashion. "Yes," he said. "Really, yes, I do."

"Then what seems to be the stickler?" asked Professor Diggins.

John thought about it. "You see, when I play I hear the music inside my head, the way I know it should sound, and I feel it . . . or something." He squirmed a little with embarrassment. "But then I start to play, and what comes out? Squeaks!" He tossed the flute into the pine needles.

Professor Diggins picked up the flute and looked at it. It caught the late afternoon sun coming through the pines, and it looked like a magic wand sparkling.

"I play the mandolin myself," said the Professor. "Not too well, but enough to please myself. I discovered, when I was learning, that the heart is the first to learn. It takes much longer for the fingers and, in the case of the flute, the lips too, to learn as well. I would guess that your heart is a very fine musician already and that it is just a bit impatient with your fingers."

John stared at him.

"In between," the Professor went on. "In between the heart learning and the music coming out the way you hear it inside, there are a few . . . um . . . well, mischievous problems to be solved."

"What sort of problems?" asked John.

"Well," Professor Diggins began after a moment's thought, "perhaps you may have noticed that the clock seems to be running backward when you practice?"

"Yes!" exclaimed John, surprised. "That's true . . . or, like it's running extra slowly, anyway."

"Anything else like that?" asked the Professor.

John thought a bit. "Well," he said, "maybe it sounds silly, but when I go to practice, lots of times, I just can't seem to find the flute or else sometimes the music books."

The Professor nodded his head sympathetically, and John went on. "And then, just when I'm supposed to start practicing, a lot of awfully important other things seem to need to be done too."

"Yes," said Professor Diggins. "That's true."

"But the hardest thing . . ." said John, and Professor Diggins looked very interested. "The hardest thing is when something makes me want to give the whole thing up."

For some reason that John did not understand right then, Professor Diggins looked extremely cheerful. "Splendid!" he said. "Just the sort of problems I had in mind." And then he got up and stretched his long legs. "What marvelous weather for dragon hunting," he said.

Around the fire after supper Jarmes, his mouth full of toasted marshmallows, said, "Professor, do you think we could have a clambake one night? Like maybe tomorrow? What do you think?"

"Mmmm," said Professor Diggins, whose mouth was also full of marshmallows. Somehow the thought of clams did not feel quite right to him. "We'll see."

"Well, that's better than 'maybe' anyhow," said Jarmes, and took another marshmallow out of the embers.

"It's not as *good* as 'maybe,'" said Lydia. "Mother always says 'maybe' when there's a pretty good chance."

"I guess you're right," said Jarmes. "Anyhow, maybe you're right."

"'Yes' is best, of course," said Orson. "But I think Lydia is right. 'Maybe' is next best."

"Well," said Professor Diggins, "That's most interesting. So then, how does the order of declining possibility go? A list would start:

> Yes
>
> Maybe
>
> We'll see.

And then what?"

"'I doubt it,'" said Mary Abby without hesitation. "'I doubt it' is the beginning of the 'no' words."

"And then, 'I don't think so,'" said John. "That's more 'no' than 'I doubt it.'"

"And then?" asked the Professor.

"Just 'no,'" said Lydia. "That's all that's left." And everyone agreed.

After a few minutes Professor Diggins could be heard humming and singing to himself and in a little while he wandered off to the bus and returned to the fire with his mandolin. "If properly urged," he said, "I might be will-

ing to play you a little song." Whereupon he was properly urged, and started to strum the wonderfully sweet mandolin.

Possibilities, possibilities, possibilities, possibilities . . .

> *"Yes" is best, "Yes" is best*
> *But next to that is "maybe";*
> *"We'll see" can sometimes grow to "yes,"*
> *But when they say "I doubt it"*
> *You're on the way to no.*
> *And next they say "I don't think so";*
> *And finally it's "no,"*
> *And finally it's "no."*

"I don't think so"
"I don't think so".
Down
Down
Down
There's nowhere else to go
But frown
And then say "no."

*Impossibilities, impossibilities, im-poss-i-bil-ities.**

---

* The music that the Professor strummed will be found at the end of this story.

CHAPTER IX

A Historic Gastronomic Event

By the next morning "We'll see" had indeed grown to "Yes." "Yes," the Professor said. "I think a clambake would be a very good kind of celebration."

"To celebrate what?" asked Lydia.

"Anything!" said the Professor, gesturing widely with his arms. "Everything! But we shall have to start right away if we are to have a clambake tonight. It's a lot of work." Lydia could be heard to sigh.

"The very first thing is for someone to run down to the road and meet the huckster and see if he will spare us one of his barrels. There are several ways to have a clambake, but for a group of our size, I favor the barrel."

Jarmes set off down the road for the barrel and for the other things they needed. Mary Abby made a careful list for him so that he wouldn't forget a thing.

"Now, for a beginning," said Professor Diggins, "we'll

have to get some clams. And there are several ways to get them, too."

"I know one," said Orson. "You go down to the edge of the water and drop a heavy rock in the sand. If there's a clam there, it spurts up a jet of water, see. Then you dig him up."

"You can do that," said Professor Diggins. "Another way is to take a clam rake and dig. I happen to have a couple of clam rakes, and I think I'll use one of those."

"I'll use the other," said John.

"Now," said Professor Diggins, more to himself than anyone else, "we're going to need a lot of seaweed—lots of it. And then the stones . . . several buckets of them. And that's just the beginning." And he said this last quite forcefully.

The Professor and John went off with the clam rakes, and Orson went straight down to the shore to start his own clam hunt. He picked up a heavy stone and dropped it. A jet of water rose at his feet. "Thar she blows!" he shouted and dug down with his hands, bringing up a sand-covered clam, which he dropped into a bucket of sea water.

Lydia, who had been standing watching Orson, suddenly bent down and picked up a rock. She threw it down into the wet sand. A jet of water rewarded her. She dug up the clam and dropped another stone. Before long she was matching Orson clam for clam.

"You're not such a bad worker, after all," said Orson.

"Oh, this is fun," said Lydia. "That's not work."

"Why?" asked Orson. "Who told you work can't be fun?"

Lydia looked surprised. "Why . . . I just know it. That's all."

"Well, don't be so sure," said Orson. "*That's* all," and he dropped a clam into the bucket.

In a couple of hours they collected nearly half a bushel of clams, and Professor Diggins said that was more than enough. "Now," he said, "they have to be washed and washed in salt water, and then we'll put them in a basket and set them out where the tide will keep them covered."

"I'll wash them," said Mary Abby, and John helped her carry the buckets of clams down to the edge of the water.

Then they all started to collect firewood. "It's almost a shame to burn some of this driftwood," Jarmes said. "I could make something nice out of it for Mother."

"What she wants," said Lydia, "is for you to bring her some pretty colored rocks and stones for her flower border. Remember?"

"Oh, yes," said Jarmes. "That's right. She did say something about that."

Orson and John started to bring in armloads of seaweed, and the Professor and Mary Abby and Jarmes collected several buckets of stones. Lydia walked along picking up stones that appealed to her for their shape and beauty and added them to the bucket.

"Now," said the Professor, "we're ready to begin."

"Begin!" Lydia said. "We've been working since early morning!"

"That was in preparation for the beginning," said the Professor. "Now, the first thing we have to do is get a great big fire going to heat these stones."

Following the Professor's directions, John put several layers of stones on the sand and Professor Diggins built a fire of driftwood on top of them. When the fire was going well, they dumped two more buckets of stones into the blaze, then more wood, then more stones, until it looked like a very bright orange wigwam.

While the stones were heating, John and Jarmes and the Professor dug a deep hole in the sand and into it they set the barrel.

"This is so mysterious," said Mary Abby. "I've never seen cooking done this way."

"Fire's about out," cried Orson after a while. "Wow! Look at those stones. They're real, real, red hot."

"They have to be hot," said the Professsor. *"They're* going to do the cooking," and he flicked a little sea water on one of the stones. It steamed and sizzled and the stones crackled.

"Now, this is the true beginning," said the Professor.

"We've had the beginning," complained Lydia. "This has to be the middle or the end."

"Well, perhaps you are right," said the Professor. "This is probably more like the beginning of the middle." Lydia looked a little upset.

"Now, Orson, if you would be good enough to put about a half inch of sea water into the bottom of this barrel, I will begin transferring some of these hot stones." So, while Orson poured sea water from one of the buckets, Professor Diggins, using a clam rake and shovel, removed about a bucket of stones from the fire and put them into the barrel, where they immediately set up a fury of steaming and crackling.

"Now," said the Professor, "if someone would please put in about three inches of seaweed, I'd be much obliged."

Mary Abby put the seaweed into the steaming barrel and the wet seaweed started to steam, too. "Watch your fingers on those hot stones," warned John.

"And now," said the Professor, who was beginning to sound like a ringmaster, "the clams!"

Jarmes and John fetched the basket of clams from the shallow water and dumped them into the steaming barrel. The aroma that came forth in the steam was so delicate and fresh and salty, it was as though the ocean itself had suddenly become a delicious food.

"Now," said the Professor, waving his arms rather wildly, "we must act speedily. More seaweed, please! And now, to top it off, those ears of corn from the huck-

ster. Some of the potatoes, please. More seaweed!" he cried to the spinning children, whose arms and legs were moving so fast, passing corn and potatoes and seaweed, that they looked rather like an odd engine.

"Now, the cover," the Professor said, shaking out a large tarpaulin and spreading it over the barrel. "And now, let's fill this hole with sand."

Everyone scrambled about covering the barrel with sand, and then they all fell back onto the beach in a heap of tiredness.

"How long does it take to cook?" asked Orson, wearily, from his spot on the sand.

"An hour and a half or two," said the Professor, also with a bit of a yawn.

"Mmmmmmmm, just time for a sort of nap maybe," said Lydia from her comfortable hollow in the sand.

"What a useful thought," said the Professor, and he said no more . . . nor did anyone.

A sand crab walking across his ankle awakened Orson. He flicked it off and sat up. "Hey!" he said, looking about. "Hey, look!"

They all sat up and rubbed their eyes. "What time is it?" asked John as Lydia said, "My, that was a good rest," and the Professor said, "Goodness, I must have dozed off."

"Look!" Orson said again and pointed to the sand. "That person with the big rubber boots has come here while we slept." And it was true. The boot marks came up out of the water, circled the sleeping group, and then went off over the sand until they disappeared.

John looked closely at the prints. "They look just like the footsteps I saw in the sand that morning on the beach," he said. "I wonder who it could be."

"He must have come and just looked at us," said Mary Abby. "Isn't that strange?"

"Not so strange," said Professor Diggins, "when you think how half a dozen bodies must look, spread out on the sand like the spokes of a wheel. Oh, my word!" and he looked at the sun, "we've come awake just in time for the best meal of our lives."

They ran back to the bus for tin plates and cups. Mary Abby made lemonade, while everyone else laid a blue checked cloth on the sand and put the tin plates about.

"I'll just melt a pot of butter on what's left of the fire," said the Professor, "and then we'll be ready to begin."

"Ooooo!" cried Lydia. *"This* can't be the beginning. We began hours ago."

"Ah, yes," said the Professor. "You're right, my dear. *This* is the beginning of the end." And he started to shovel the sand away from the barrel. They carefully swept the rest of the sand from the tarpaulin and lifted it. A wave of steam and a light, mouth-aching aroma came from the barrel. Then off with the top layer of seaweed, and then the hot corn and potatoes were laid onto a big platter and put on the tablecloth. Then the clams—steaming, open, and luscious—were brought in a big pan to the improvised table.

"There is just this one thing about the etiquette of clambakes," said Professor Diggins. "It is extremely bad manners to use a knife and fork. This is the way," and his hand dived into a pile of clams. He removed the clam from its shell, dipped it into the pot of melted butter, and throwing back his head, dropped it into his mouth. A look of quiet delight came over his face. "Ahhh, such a beginning!" he said. "I beg your pardon," he said to Lydia. "Such an end!"

Everyone followed his etiquette lesson and dived into the clams, dunked them in butter, dropped them into opened mouths, and even imitated the Professor as to the expression of delight.

The corn was rolled in butter and salted, and the potatoes, steamed to fluffy perfection, were treated the same way. Clams, butter, potatoes, butter, corn, butter.

"I've never been so buttery," said Mary Abby. "But it's nice."

Suddenly Jarmes whispered, "Look, who's that?" and he pointed to a spot way down the beach where a small figure could be seen walking along the edge of the water.

"Whoever it is," said the Professor, "ask him, for heaven's sake, to come and help us finish these clams. I've done all I can."

Jarmes got up and ran down the beach and they all watched. "Hi!" he yelled as he approached the little man. The man seemed to see him for the first time then and turned on his heels, and walking very fast, disappeared behind the dunes. "Hi!" Jarmes yelled. "I wanted to ask you to the clambake." But the little man didn't answer. And then Jarmes saw the footprints. He kept his eyes on the sand all the way back to the clambake.

"He's the one," he said. "The one with the bootprints. The one that came and looked at us."

"What did he say when you asked him?" asked Lydia.

"He didn't answer," said Jarmes. "He just turned and walked away."

"How impolite!" said Mary Abby, and she started to pass around a bag of licorice for dessert. Everyone took one except Orson.

"No, thanks," he said. "I've had enough candy for a while."

"Nobody ever has enough candy," said Jarmes, chewing the licorice.

"Why you haven't even had *any*," said Lydia, trying to talk with licorice stuck to the roof of her mouth.

"I feel as though I have," said Orson, and then he turned to the Professor. "You were right," he said, "I'm going to start tapering off."

As the light disappeared they gathered up the clam-shells and buried them in the hole they had cooked in. They covered the ashes of the fire and smoothed and raked over the whole area.

"No one would know," said the Professor, "that this has been just recently the scene of a historic gastronomic event."

As they turned toward the bus, and bed, Mary Abby cried, "Look, a shooting star!"

"Make a wish!" cried Lydia. "Quickly!"

Mary Abby squeezed her eyes shut tightly, and an intent look came on her face as she wished so hard that no one could doubt that it was an important wish.

"That one should come true," said the Professor.

"What makes you think so?" asked Mary Abby.

"When you want something so very much," the Professor said, "you don't usually stand around just waiting for luck. You help a little . . . a lot."

"There goes another!" cried Orson.

"Ah, the summer sky . . ." sighed the Professor as he gazed at it, "so familiar that to look at it is to walk down the street of one's home town."

"It's not familiar to me," said Jarmes. "All I know is the Big Dipper."

"You need to do a bit of stargazing, that's all," said Professor Diggins.

"Could we spend some time stargazing tonight?" asked Orson.

"Well, not tonight," said the Professor. "I must confess to excessive sleepiness tonight. How about tomorrow?"

Everyone said Yes to that; and necks craned, eyes on the sky, they backed into the bus for the night.

CHAPTER X

How to Make a Sky

But the next morning it rained, and even though it stopped raining by midday, it stayed foggy all afternoon. Orson cast a pessimistic eye on the sky. "There won't be any stars tonight," he said.

"Don't be silly," said Lydia. "Where would they go?"

"Oh, they're *there*," Orson said, "but they'll be hidden behind the clouds. We won't be able to see them to gaze at them." And he went off to his laboratory to work on his snail research. He had found that racing them was the only means of testing the snails that he could measure. He spent a good deal of time tempting them with whatever came to hand, but as yet he had not discovered anything that the snails seemed really to *want*. He was confident, however, that when he did, he could encourage them to hurry.

Lydia's sun porch was not much use on a cloudy day,

except as a place to lean out into the water and look for small fish. After a rain was a good time for this, and Lydia spent some time at it before she got tired and wandered off to visit Mary Abby.

Mary Abby was in her sewing room mending Orson's shirt, which had gotten ripped on a rock. "There won't be any stars tonight," said Lydia, but Mary Abby was worrying about this without any help from Lydia.

Jarmes, with an armful of shell bracelets, came in to have a button sewed on, and while Mary Abby was doing it he said, "Won't be any stars tonight," and Lydia and Mary Abby said mournfully, "We know."

Professor Diggins and John came to join them after spending an hour working out duets for the flute and mandolin. "Almost ready to make our musical debut, I think," said the Professor. "What's everyone so blue about?" he asked, looking at their disconsolate faces.

"There won't be any stars tonight," said Lydia. And then they all went out onto the beach and considered the sky glumly.

At nightfall they were still searching the sky for a glimmer, but there was none. Professor Diggins regarded their disappointed faces with a certain amount of surprise and, it would seem, pleasure. "Well," he said, "in dealing with people as eager as you, we cannot wait upon chance. We shall have to make our own sky. If you will go to the grove, I will be out in a minute. I have a sky around here somewhere."

It was beginning to drizzle again and the children went to the protection of the pine grove and waited while the Professor searched the bus for something. Suddenly he cried, "Ah, here it is!" and came loping out of the bus and joined them in the grove. In the darkness it was a bit hard to see just what he was carrying, but when he reached them he cried, *"Voilà,* the celestial hemisphere!" and he opened an enormous black umbrella over his head. Then he reached into his pocket for a piece of chalk, and gathering the children under the umbrella, he began to draw stars on the canopy over their heads. "Here," he said, making a cross with the chalk, "is the place to begin—the North Star."

"And that's at the top of the Big Dipper," said Jarmes. "And that's all I know."

"Enough for a beginning," said the Professor. "If you would be good enough to make the Big Dipper, it would free my arms to hold up the sky." So Jarmes started to mark off the stars of the Big Dipper with the Professor's suggestions and advice about the exact position of each star as it would appear in the sky on this day, at this hour, in the month of August.

"A little to the left," the Professor would say. "Not quite so far apart." And then, "Ah, nearly perfect!"

"Now here's the thing," he said, gazing up into the umbrella. "The sky's so big and changes all the time, and there is so much to learn that the problem becomes what to show you first. I think the thing you want to do is to look up into the sky and see something familiar."

"That's it," said John.

"Well, then," said the Professor, "let's do it the way the Greeks did. Now the Greeks would look at the sky and the stars seemed to be in natural groups, called constellations, and they would see people or animals in these constellations and great stories were told about them. For instance, the Big Dipper that Jarmes has put into the sky is part of a constellation called Ursa Major, the Great Bear, because the Greeks thought those stars grouped together looked like an enormous bear. And then, beside it, of course, is Ursa Minor."

"The Little Bear," said Orson.

"Now here," said the Professor, after taking the chalk and quickly putting in Ursa Minor, "we have Cassiopeia, the woman in the chair, right across from the Big Dipper on the opposite side of the North Star. And here, high in the sky, is Pegasus, the winged horse. And a way over here is Andromeda. Ah, she is one of my favorites . . . a lovely Greek girl rescued from a sea monster by gallant Perseus. . . ." And for a moment Professor Diggins was quite carried away by the memory of Andromeda. Then he went on to show them the constellations of Orion the Hunter, and Taurus the Bull; and around each of the chalked groups of stars, the children found, if they squinted, that the people and animals seemed to take shape. Gathered under the big umbrella, the firelight illuminating it, the children watched with pleasure as it became transformed from a black umbrella into a summer sky.

"And that's about it for tonight," said Professor Diggins. "We can't take in too much sky watching or we become dazzled."

"But what's that star?" asked Jarmes, pointing to a small glimmering spot in the umbrella.

The Professor squinted at it. "Hmmm, that's not familiar," and he looked at it more closely. "Ah, Jarmes, *you* are the astronomer among us. You have discovered a new star called the Hole in the Umbrella."

CHAPTER XI

A Man
in the Storm

Lydia was looking closely at her reflection in a tide pool among the rocks.

"Lydia, stop admiring yourself and come and help me with these starfish," called Jarmes.

"I'm not admiring myself," said Lydia, without taking offense. "I'm just pretending that my reflection is a mermaid. I'm a mermaid stranded in the tide pool, and I have to wait until the tide comes in to set me free." Jarmes laughed.

"Don't laugh," said Lydia. "I'm positively frantic caught there like that, all by myself. Of course I don't know that the tide will come in and free me. I think I may be trapped in the little pool forever. Oh, Jarmes, isn't that frightening!" Lydia was quite caught up in her own story.

"Frightening," said Jarmes. "Come on over and help

collect these starfish. There are lots of them today and
the Professor needs them."

"Ooooo!" cried Lydia. "Do you think the Professor
would like a mermaid for the salt water tank?"

Jarmes growled, but he was used to Lydia.

And just then he saw the Man-with-the-Boots. "Hey,
look!" he whispered, pointing. Lydia looked up then and
together they watched the little man as he walked slowly
across the sand. His gait was strange and a bit pigeon-
toed. His manner was odd. He would walk a step and
then look up and then look down and then turn around,
or some variation of these acts. And now and then he
would pick something up and put it in his pocket. As he

came closer, quite unaware of his observers, Jarmes and Lydia could see that he was dressed in tweed knickerbockers, the kind Jarmes said their grandfather used to wear to play golf. These were met near the knee by enormous rolled rubber boots. His jacket matched his trousers and Lydia said that showed he was neat. His thin, very pale face was partly hidden and well shaded from the sun by a very large pith helmet—the kind used by hunters in deepest Africa.

"Is he old or young?" asked Lydia.

"Oldish," said Jarmes. "Or maybe middleish."

When the man had passed them and disappeared down the beach, Jarmes and Lydia scrambled off the rocks and went to examine the sand. "That's him, all right," said Jarmes, pointing to the bootprints. "Those are the same prints."

"But what was he doing?" asked Lydia. "I was looking right at him and I couldn't tell what he was doing."

Back at the bus Jarmes and Lydia described the Man-with-the-Boots and they all spent some time that evening discussing who he might be and what he might be doing.

"Maybe," said John, "he is an old shipwrecked sailor and he comes back here and sort of goes over the ground, remembering."

"No," said Mary Abby, "that's too much like a story. He's probably just an old tramp who lives in the woods and he goes around the beach looking for things to eat."

"That's right," said Lydia; "he was picking up things."

"We pick up things too," said Orson, "and we're not tramps. I'll bet I picked up a hundred sand crabs for the salt water tank today."

"Well, he put the things in his pockets," said Jarmes, "so I'll bet they weren't sand crabs," and Jarmes jumped up and started hopping about and beating himself with his arms as he imagined his pockets full of sand crabs.

Just who the Man-with-the-Boots was and what he was doing was not to be discovered . . . until the next day.

It started with Mary Abby washing out their clothes. It was not a good day for hanging up clothes because it was overcast and windy, but Mary Abby hoped the wind would dry the clothes before it rained. She bent to pick up a shirt from the basket and was just clipping it onto the line when she noticed that the first shirt was gone.

"Oh, dear!" she cried, "that's awfully strange!" and clipped on the shirt she held in her hand. Then when she was hanging up the third shirt, she saw that the second shirt was gone. And suddenly the wind caught at her dress, blew it wildly, then swept down and picked up two more shirts from the basket and carried them off like fall leaves over the beach.

John saw the shirts fly by and cried, "For Pete's sake!" and yelled, "Jarmes! Orson! Come on!" and started down the beach after the shirts, nearly catching up and then having them whipped from under his hand.

Orson caught two shirts, then John and Jarmes caught the others. And suddenly Orson panted, "Look there! The Man-with-the-Boots! Just look at him!"

The Man-with-the-Boots was tearing around in circles like a whirlwind, catching at the air and catching at the ground, tucking things into his trouser pockets and into his jacket. Catching and snatching like an elderly dervish.

"He looks like he's going to cry," exclaimed Lydia, who, with Mary Abby, had joined in the shirt chase.

"Let's go see what he's doing," said Jarmes, starting off, and they all followed him, the wind whipping them as they ran.

"They're *feathers!*" cried Lydia. "They're feathers he's catching!" and she caught a feather and ran up to the frantic man. He looked at her for an instant with strange wide eyes and took the feather without a word.

"Here's one!" cried Jarmes. "And here's another." And he gave them to the Man-with-the-Boots. Then all the children were swooping and dipping and grabbing, and before long the man had dozens of long feathers in his hands and sticking out of his pockets.

"That's all I can find!" screamed Lydia over the wind. And just then a sheet of rain came down upon them.

"It's getting awful! Let's go back to the bus," cried Mary Abby, and she turned and started pushing against the wind, making very little headway.

John took the arm of the Man-with-the-Boots. "It's going to be a bad storm," he yelled. "You'd better come with us. You'll be drenched."

"No, no. I can go home," protested the man, but he couldn't push his way against the wind either.

"Look here," said John, "we'll form a line. Then each person can push the one in front. Take him, too," he said, indicating the man. "Jarmes, you lead. I'll push from the back."

So they formed a long, strong line that worked quite well. They made very good progress, with only one minor mishap when the Man-with-the-Boots stumbled and fell to the sand, twisting his ankle as he did so. But they had him on his feet and the line reassembled in short order.

They started trudging against the wind again, a little slower now to accommodate the man's slight limp.

At about that moment Professor Diggins had reached the end of some long and involved notes about the creatures in the tanks, and he raised his head from his notebook. It was then that he noticed for the first time that the bus was rocking furiously, that there was a howling wind, and that rain was dripping on his head from a leak in the roof.

"Good gracious!" said the Professor, and went to the door of the bus and pushed it open. He was blown back to his chair. The children! he thought. Where can they be? and he had just struggled back to the door when the line of children puffed and pushed up to the bus and in through the open door, with a rather confused Man-with-the-Boots sandwiched between Lydia and Orson.

"Well!" exclaimed the Professor. *"There* you are!"

"We've brought a guest," panted Lydia. "Professor Diggins, may I present Mr. . . .Mr. . . ." and she looked inquiringly at the little man. "I'm sorry," she said. "We just call you the Man-with-the-Boots."

The man looked at her strangely. "Boots," he said. "Mmmm, boots."

"So very delighted to meet you, Mr. Boots," said the Professor. "Do please make yourself comfortable while we fix a bit of hot cocoa all around. Charming of you to come and call on us, and on such a nasty day."

Mr. Boots was limping rather badly now and John helped him over to a chair. Orson kneeled and unlaced his shoe. Mr. Boots made protesting sounds, but when Orson said, "Your ankle is really swollen," the man allowed Orson to place it on another chair, muttering what sounded a bit like "Thank you."

Mary helped the Professor with the spirit stove and they made a cheerful pot of cocoa, which they all drank quietly while the wind howled and the rain gathered in the pots of herbs the Professor had placed under the leak in the roof.

Everyone had certain thoughts to think for a while,

and there wasn't much conversation. But then the Professor looked up and said, "You have an interest in feathers, Mr. Boots?"

Mr. Boots looked flustered for a moment, and then following Professor Diggins' gaze, he grabbed at his pockets which were bulging with feathers. Then he said softly, "Yes. Yes. I have a great interest in feathers." And then, as they were all looking at him with strict attention, he added, "But, of course, only gull feathers."

"Ah," said the Professor as if that made everything quite clear. "Gull feathers. You make something out of gull feathers."

"No," said Mr. Boots. "I don't make anything. I save them." And then he added, "I sort them." And then suddenly getting quite bold, he spoke with a kind of brave thrust of his chest. "I have," he declared, "the largest, if not the only, collection of gull feathers in the world!"

"Indeed!" exclaimed Professor Diggins. "Fancy that! All kinds of gulls—herring gull, glaucous gull, Iceland gull, great black-backed gull . . . all the *Larinae?* Laughing gull—*Larus atricilla?*"

"Most," said Mr. Boots, looking surprised and pleased with the Professor's interest and knowledge. "Most. Though sometimes it is hard or impossible to tell just which gull they're from. But I try."

"Where do you keep them all?" asked John.

"Why do you want to know?" said Mr. Boots, suddenly narrowing his eyes and looking suspiciously at John.

"I just wondered, that's all," said John, shrugging.

Mr. Boots continued to look suspicious but he said, "I have a couple of rooms for them."

"A couple of rooms!" said Jarmes. "Doesn't that crowd you?"

"No," said Mr. Boots, "I'm not crowded. But then I don't really require much room myself. I don't have many needs." And then, as if finally he had gotten into the habit of speaking, he talked more easily. "I'm a loner . . . like the gull. In fact . . ." and his voice wandered off.

"In fact?" asked Lydia politely.

"In fact," said Mr. Boots, "I sometimes wish I *were* a gull. I should be free, graceful, above the ground . . . never beset by people."

"Do people beset you now?" asked Orson.

Mr. Boots frowned. "Yes," he said. And he said no more but drew himself down into his collar, rather like a turtle, and they all tried not to stare at him.

The wind continued to howl and rock the bus, and the rain looked like Christmas tinsel on the windowpanes. Professor Diggins was the first to break the silence.

Clearly he had been thinking about what Mr. Boots had
said.

"Yes," he said. "I think you're right, Mr. Boots. If I
could be anything other than human, just for a little
while, I think I should like to be a bird." Mr. Boots
looked up with interest. The Professor continued
thoughtfully, "Not necessarily a lovable bird, like a wren
or a sparrow. No, I think I should be a capable, durable
bird, like the osprey, perhaps. The prey and the predator
of few." And then he returned to his thinking.

"I should be a beaver," said Mary Abby, "because they

live in such lovely houses on the river and are so busy and clean and neat."

"I'd be an ant," said Orson.

"An ant!" everyone exclaimed. "Why?"

"Just because nobody else probably wants to be one," said Orson. "Beside, I understand they are rather wonderful."

"I would be a fish," said Lydia, "and lie on my back in the sea all day."

Jarmes laughed. "If you lie on your back when you're a fish, you're a dead fish."

"Oh, very well, I shall just swim about quietly, looking at the shells and seaweed and doing nothing."

"You do very well at that right now," said Jarmes. And then he said, "I'm sorry, but you are a lazy thing, Lydia."

"Oh, I know it!" said Lydia, and she smiled so pleasantly that everyone laughed.

 *A Revelation*

The rain stopped suddenly, as though someone had turned off the spigot, but the wind continued
strong. Mr. Boots looked at the windows and then at his
swollen ankle. "I have to get home," he said, but Professor Diggins said the wind was still strong enough to
blow him over.

John cleared his throat then and said, "Mr. Boots, sir,
may I ask you a question?"

Mr. Boots looked nervously at John from under pale
furry eyebrows. He took a deep breath and said, "Well,
all right. What is it, then?" in a not too friendly way.

John was not encouraged, but he went on. "Well, I was
just going to say, sir, that I noticed your bootprints on
the beach one morning and they seemed to come right
out of the ocean. And I couldn't see exactly how they
could have, because there wasn't any path of footsteps
going in."

Mr. Boots was suspicious again. "You were following me."

"No, sir," said John, "not following *you*. It's just I was surprised to see the bootprints, so I followed *them*."

"Hmmm." Mr. Boots suddenly seemed to take an interest in the question. "Came out of the sea, did you say? No path in? What time of day was that?"

"About six in the morning, I think," said John.

"Day of the month?" asked Mr. Boots.

"Let's see," John thought aloud. "That was the day that mmmm . . . and that was the day before . . . mmmm. I think it would have been about the fifteenth," he said.

"The fifteenth. Ah!" Mr. Boots looked up from his thinking. He looked at the faces all focused on him. "Are you *all* interested in this?"

"Oh, yes!" they exclaimed.

"Imagine that!" Mr. Boots murmured. "This isn't a trick, is it? You're not trying to get . . . well, to get something else from me?"

"What else?" asked Lydia, interested.

"Well, just anything else," said Mr. Boots.

"Of course not," said Orson.

"Well, all right," said Mr. Boots. "How about this? On the fifteenth of this month the tide was coming in toward high at about six, I should guess, if I remember right."

"Just so," said Professor Diggins.

"So," said Mr. Boots, "if I had gone down the shore to the point where the beach is narrow and then walked into the water, as I sometimes do, and walked along in the water to the point where you saw the bootprints come out . . ."

"I have it," cried Orson. "The tide was coming in, right?" As everyone nodded, he went on. "When the tide came in it erased the path your footsteps made going into the water at the narrow beach, but it left some of them where you came out where the beach was wider."

"That's what I was thinking," agreed Mr. Boots.

"Well that's settled then," said John. "It's been on my mind."

"Is that all!" complained Jarmes. "I thought it would be something more—more . . ."

"Mystical," said Lydia.

And then quite suddenly the storm seemed to get out of breath. It puffed a bit for a time, but the bus stopped rocking. And then it was still. They listened expectantly but it didn't start again. Then everyone began to talk.

Mr. Boots said, "I must be going," and stood up just as Mary Abby said, "I nearly threw up, it was so rough," and Professor Diggins said, "Well, let's see how the bean vines made out." And then quite suddenly Mr. Boots sat down again.

"Oh, dear," he said, wrinkling his face, "I seem to have hurt my ankle more than I thought. Oh, dear."

"Well, my good fellow," the Professor said, "you just bunk right here with us until you feel fit to leave."

"Oh, yes," said Jarmes. "You may have my cot and I'll bunk in with Orson."

"No, no," protested Mr. Boots, "I must go home. I must go home. I have things I must do."

"In that case," said Professor Diggins, "we will take you there."

"No, no," cried Mr. Boots. "I never have anyone visit."

"But Mr. Boots," said Lydia, "we don't care what kind of housekeeper you are."

"Look how simply we are living," said Mary Abby. "We have no luxuries except for Mrs. Diggins' china."

Mr. Boots stared at her. "No, no," he moaned. "You don't understand."

But Mr. Boots was in no condition to protest, and if he wanted to get home he had no choice but to accept help. Jarmes, John, and Professor Diggins made a comfortable carrying chair for him by putting two pillows on a straight chair and tying them with bathrobe belts. Mary Abby bandaged his swollen ankle with a torn dish towel just the way she had been taught in first aid class. "I'm glad now I practiced on the banister so much," she said.

Then they lifted Mr. Boots onto the chair, and with

John and Professor Diggins on the back legs, Mary and Jarmes on the front legs, and Lydia and Orson leading the way, they lifted the chair into the air and started out across the sand. Following Mr. Boots' directions, they went way down the beach, crossed the dunes, traveled a

way through the scrubby field, turned left out onto a rocky promontory, and suddenly behind some enormous pine trees they saw the house.

"Is that it?" asked Mary Abby. "That?"

"That's it," said Mr. Boots weakly.

"But it's a mansion!" cried John. "A regular mansion!"

"I know," said Mr. Boots, "a regular mansion."

And then they were at the great, carved oak front door. Jarmes reached up to lift the knocker, but he jumped back before he completed the action. "Oh, gosh! Look at that knocker!" he said in a whisper.

"Oh!" cried Lydia. "It's a dragon! A really awful-looking dragon."

"Mmmm," said Professor Diggins, peering closely at the enormous iron door knocker. "Interesting. I wonder," he said, half to himself, "if there is a *real* dragon to hunt here?" And before anyone could ask the Professor what he meant, John went bravely up to the horrible door knocker and gave it a tug. That took a great deal of strength, and when it fell back it sounded like thunder. Mary Abby and Lydia grabbed each other's arms and Lydia said, "If the Professor weren't with us, I'd run!"

"Oh, so would I," said Mary Abby.

And in a moment the enormous door was swung open by an elegant man who could be nothing but a butler. "Oh, I'm so glad to see you, sir. We've been so worried about you. Cook, in fact, is nearly beside herself. What has happened, sir?"

"Oh, do stop going on, please, Moffitt," said Mr. Boots. "I've turned my ankle, that's all. Thank you for your concern," he added, as the butler looked a bit hurt.

"Well, you're back safe and sound, anyway," said Moffitt. "That's really all that matters, Mr. Pym."

"Mr. Pym!" said Lydia, as they set the carrying chair down.

"Mr. Pym!" said Jarmes. "But that's right, we really just made up Boots, didn't we?"

"Mr. Pym!" said Professor Diggins. "Surely you are not the Davenport Pym the University is urging to give them a million dollars?"

"The same," said Mr. Pym sadly. "The same Mr. Pym that *everyone* and his sister and brother are urging to give them *something!*" and he thrust out his bottom lip and started to sulk.

"What shall I do with these . . . um . . . persons, sir?" asked the butler quietly of Mr. Pym.

"What sort of thing did you have in mind?" asked Mr. Pym. "It's been so long since we've had visitors, I rather forget what one *does* do with them."

"Well," said Moffitt, "since they were kind enough to help you home, perhaps I could bring them around to the kitchen and cook could give them a cup of tea."

"Oh," said Mr. Pym, "that sort of thing! Mmmm.

Well, the kitchen isn't right. Much too . . . ummm . . . picnickish. These are my guests. We shall have to do something more elaborate."

"Guests, sir?" asked Moffitt.

"Yes, indeed."

"Well, sir, in that case," and Moffitt's eyes began to sparkle, "would you wish to go so far as to have dinner in the dining room? Cook, I dare say, could whip up something. She hasn't cooked anything but lamb chops in so long she would be happy to try her skills again."

"Ah, dinner!" said Mr. Pym. "Yes, something like that. It *would* be nice to have guests to dinner . . . a change from eating on a tray in my room. Perhaps we could even have," and he took a deep breath, "a party!"

"A party! Oh, sir!" Moffitt's eyes were truly alight. "Yes, sir. In two hours' time, sir. Just leave it to cook and me." And he was off.

Mr. Pym turned back to the room and cleared his throat. "It gives me pleasure to invite all of you to attend a party this evening at six," he said.

"A party!" they all exclaimed.

"Oh, yes," said Mr. Pym, trying to sound calm, as if he always had parties and on two hours' notice.

"But we have nothing to wear," moaned Lydia.

"Nothing but beach clothes," said Mary Abby.

"Hmmm," said Mr. Pym. "Well, I'll tell you what.

There are twenty-five bedrooms upstairs with twenty-five bureaus and twenty-five closets full of clothes that belonged to people who lived in this house over the years. I shouldn't be a bit surprised if there were some party clothes up there. Just make yourselves quite comfortable and help yourselves. My room is down here. I'll see you in the conservatory at a quarter of six. And he limped off into the darkened hallway.

"Is it all right, Professor?" asked John. "Can we really just go and help ourselves?"

"It's certainly a bit unusual," said Professor Diggins, "but if Mr. Pym says we may, it is quite all right. I expect I'd best brush myself up a bit and look for some shoes."

"Oh, then let's go!" cried Lydia, and she was off in the lead, out into the hall, followed closely by Orson, Jarmes,

John, and Mary Abby, all racing up the wide circular staircase, their bare feet feeling wonderfully cold on the brightly polished dark wood steps. They came to a halt in the big upper hallway, where corridors shot off dimly in four directions.

"I'll go this way," said Jarmes, setting off to the left.

"I'm going right in here," said Lydia, peeking into a bedroom into which the late afternoon sun was shining. "It looks cheery."

And they each chose a room and disappeared behind its heavy door. In a moment Orson tugged open the door of his room. "I've got a girl's room," he complained to no one in particular, since there was no one in the hallway, and he chose another room which proved to be quite suitable.

Mary Abby had to pick another room too. "This person is entirely too fat for me," she said. And after just a bit more shifting about, a great deal of quiet fell over the upper floor of the Pym mansion.

But downstairs in the kitchen, pantry, and dining room it was another matter entirely. Moffitt and Mrs. Moffitt, the cook, were all but leaping about with delight.

"Can you do it?" asked Moffitt. "In two hours, I mean."

"I could do it in two minutes if I had to," said Mrs.

Moffitt, "and have a minute left over. "Quick, get those fillets out of the freezer."

"How is my formal livery?" asked Moffitt as he took the beautiful fillets of beef out of the deep freeze.

"You know your livery is always pressed and ready," said Mrs. Moffitt as she lit the oven with one hand and sifted flour with the other. "What are they like?"

"An odd lot," said Moffitt, "but they're *people*, that's the thing. Real people! Five minor children and an old gentleman. But they have manners."

"Quickly," said Mrs. Moffitt, "go down to the cellar and get me some mushrooms, and then come and peel me a dozen potatoes."

"Ahhh," said Moffitt, breathing deeply as Mrs. Moffitt measured vanilla into the batter she was mixing, "this kitchen is beginning to smell beautiful already."

"Stop mooning," said Mrs. Moffitt briskly. "Mush-rooms!"

CHAPTER XIII

All About Dragons

The enormous clock in the upstairs hall struck the quarter hour and all the bedroom doors opened. Then there appeared from each doorway a creature so different from the one that had gone in that they could only stare at each other in silent admiration.

Jarmes spoke first, if you could call it speaking. "Whoop!" he said.

And then everyone was looking at Lydia. She was wearing a stiff white organdy dress with great full skirts over enormous crinoline petticoats. It looked a few sizes too big, but she had put a safety pin or two in useful places. "I keep losing my shoes," she said and pulled up her skirt a bit to show high-heeled red velvet pumps. "I've put paper in the toes."

"Charming!" said the Professor. "And you see, I have found some fine shoes, too," and he indicated his feet shod in shining black patent leather pumps. To complete his dinner outfit, he had added a black satin waistcoat and a fresh bow tie. "And now let's look at the rest of you," he said.

Orson stepped forward in a dark green velvet suit with a bright fuschia cummerbund spanning his ample stomach. "Simply marvelous!" said the Professor, and he turned to look at Jarmes. "Ah, a masterpiece of sartorial originality!" he exclaimed as he examined Jarmes' ensemble. It consisted of a very sporty pair of striped baseball pants, an extremely handsome tailcoat, and an only slightly lopsided top hat.

Then John stepped out of the shadowy doorway and Lydia gasped, "He's a soldier!"

"Well, well!" Professor Diggins said. "So he is! And a soldier of the Civil War at that."

"It's long," John said, "but I made it fit." And he pointed to the trouser legs, rolled up, as were the cuffs of the sleeves. The cap slid far down on his forehead.

And just then Mary Abby stepped quietly out of her room and into a pool of light at the head of the stairs. Everybody gasped.

Then Lydia said, "Oh, Mary Abby, you're *beautiful!*" And she was. In the closet of her room she had found a pale blue silk gown with a high empire waist gathered on a thin velvet ribbon. The dress reached to her ankles, which were tied up in the ribbons of white ballet slippers.

She had piled her hair high on her head and in it was a white wax rose. And more than that, there was an extraordinary glow about her that was only partly from the late afternoon sun that lighted the hall.

"Thank you," said Mary Abby, blushing, but gracefully. "Thank you very much. It feels very . . . well . . . unexpected."

The Professor cleared his throat. "A really handsome group," he said. "But let's hurry down to the conservatory, or we'll commit the unpardonable gaffe of being late to dinner." And he led the way down the winding stairway. The children followed—Lydia, picking up her crinolines daintily; John, marching; Mary Abby, walking with careful, measured steps and feeling entirely beautiful, queenly, and wonderfully impractical; Jarmes, swaggering just a bit, standing aside courteously to let her by; and Orson, when the others had gotten a good start, skidding down the banister on his velvet pants.

Well, that was a party!

The table in the great old dining room was set with the whitest linens, the brightest silver, the tallest candles, and the clearest crystal. The chandelier above the table sparkled with a hundred tiny lights. In front of each place was a little silver basket of candies and nuts. Moffitt was standing straight as a soldier in his handsome dark red livery, holding a chair for Mary Abby, then Lydia.

"Oh, my!" gasped Mary Abby.

Lydia said, "It's just like a grown-up's party."

Mr. Pym looked very small, but nevertheless very impressive, sitting at the head of the table in the enormous high-backed chair. His pale face was brightened by his cheeks, now rosy with excitement, and his blue eyes spar-kled as if it were his birthday.

The first course was served in tall iced glasses and seemed to be some sort of orangey ice in a clear red liquid.

Lydia asked, "What is it?"

Jarmes said, "It's not polite to ask. Just eat it."

But Moffitt leaned over and whispered in Lydia's ear, "It's cranberry shrub, miss. Cook makes the fresh cran-berry juice and freezes the orange ice herself." And it was delicious—a cold, bright, sweet-and-sour taste that sharpened the appetite.

Next was a delicate cress soup and then Moffitt brought the plates of beautifully grilled fillets of beef, decorated with frilled mushrooms, slices of candied car-rots tied up like gift packages with bows made of pi-miento, and tiny browned potato balls the size of mar-bles, crisp and buttery.

Moffitt tried not to smile from ear to ear, because but-lers are not supposed to, but he was unsuccessful. He looked like a man who had just won a lottery. Mrs. Moffitt peeked around the swinging door and watched their faces as they ate her beautiful dinner.

And then dessert. Moffitt carried in an enormous silver tray filled to its edges with petits fours iced in pale pink, pale green, pale yellow, white, chocolate, and even a few blue, and decorated with iced roses, leaves, and violets. Each petit four had a tiny white candle in its center and the silver tray reflected the twinkling lights.

First they all drew in their breath and gasped with pleasure, and then they let it out and blew out the candles. Everyone had a petit four of each color. Mary Abby said she was beginning to feel like a rainbow inside. Lydia, taking the last blue bite, said, "I have never, ever, had enough petits fours before today!"

And when they all had finally fallen back into their chairs with a partly eaten petit four in front of each of them, Professor Diggins said, "Mr. Pym, I wonder if you could answer a question."

"I can try," said Mr. Pym. "I'm not too good at quizzes, though."

"What I am wondering," said the Professor, "is how you happen to have chosen a dragon for a door knocker?"

"Oh, I found it in one of the cellars many, many years ago," said Mr. Pym. "I put it there because I thought it might discourage some of the people."

"Ah, yes, dragons usually do," said the Professor.

"Which people?" asked Lydia.

Mr. Pym scowled. "The people who are always asking for things." Mr. Pym's face grew rather angry. "The people who pretend to like me because I am rich—children begging at Halloween, salesmen who think I will spend my money on anything, universities asking for new gymnasiums."

"But what about your friends?" asked John. "You don't want to frighten them."

"I've never had friends," said Mr. Pym. "People don't like me. They only come around because I am rich. They always want something."

"But we don't want anything," cried Mary Abby, "and we are your friends."

"We didn't even know you *had* anything," said John gruffly.

"We thought you were a tramp, living in the woods in a shack," said Lydia.

"Hush, Lydia! That's not polite," Jarmes said.

Mr. Pym looked at her closely. "Did you? Did you *really?*" he asked.

"Really," said Lydia, and all the children agreed.

"And you helped me and everything just because . . ."

"Because you needed help," said Orson. "That's why we helped you."

"Not because of anything else," said Mr. Pym, reviewing the matter for himself. "Not because of my enormous wealth and influence. And you are having dinner with me because . . ."

"Just because we like you," said Lydia.

Mr. Pym smiled with pleasure. "Isn't that splendid!" he said.

"Ahhh," said Professor Diggins, "then that dragon at the door seems to represent not so much a door knocker as a *real* dragon."

"What do you mean *real* dragon?" asked Mr. Pym. "I didn't think there were such things as real dragons."

"Oh, heavens, yes!" said Professor Diggins. "It's one of the things that occupies my thoughts constantly—how people continue to believe that there are *not*. I keep calling it to my students' attention, over and over again, at the University." His voice saddened a little. "But with some it is hard to make the point. They have a great many distractions, you know, and then we are not really set up to study dragons."

"But," began Mr. Pym, still confused, "I really don't see . . . that is . . ." and his voice trailed off.

"You see," Professor Diggins said, "real dragons stand in the way of progress . . . keep us from doing our best, for instance. Why, these young people, here," he said, turning to the children, "have been dragon hunting all summer long . . . and with singular success, I may say."

John's eyes suddenly widened. Orson started to smile and Professor Diggins smiled back. "Goodness, yes," the Professor said, "there are all kinds of dragons."

"Well," said Lydia helpfully, "I know there is the kind

that keeps people from going around the mountain with a crock of butter."

Mr. Pym looked at her with a puzzled expression, but John said excitedly, "And there's the kind that keeps you from practicing the flute."

"And the kind that makes some people afraid of the dark!" exclaimed Orson.

"Those are dragons!" said Jarmes with surprise. "The kind that makes people forget things?"

"You said it!" said the Professor.

"Ohhh!" cried Lydia, "The kind that makes some people a little lazy!"

"And the kind," said Mary Abby slowly, "that keeps some people from knowing what they can truly be."

The puzzled look was disappearing from Mr. Pym's face. "I see," he said. And then he said, "The kind that makes some people distrust everyone and put up scary door knockers."

"Oh, bravo!" said Professor Diggins. "*Just* that kind. You see," he went on, speaking to Mr. Pym, "the first problem always is to recognize them as dragons. Then we can try and fight them. And if we all just get used to fighting the small dragons as we find them, there will be fewer larger ones later. But, in any case, we are in condition, so to speak. We are ready for the big ones that *are* there. And, of course, you see, there are more than our own personal dragons. Anything . . . anything at all that stands in the way of knowledge, of understanding, of moving upward, of acting in the right, may very well be a dragon."

The Professor sighed. "Much as I would love to keep

my eyes on the tiny creatures of the sea and shore, as long as there are dragons about, I must hunt for them too."

Mr. Pym looked grave. "My dear Professor," he said, "how glad I am that you do hunt them, and how I wish you could have told me all this years ago. Moffitt! Moffitt!" he called. And when Moffitt appeared, he said, "For a beginning, please have the door knocker removed in the morning."

As they all rose from the table, Professor Diggins said to Mr. Pym. "I wonder if you would be kind enough to allow us to see your collection of feathers?"

Mr. Pym blushed with pleasure. "Oh, would you really like to?" he asked. "You're the first person who has ever asked to see it. It is surprising how few people are interested in gull feathers. Come this way, please."

Limping slightly, he led them out of the dining room, through the great hallway, into a back corridor, around two turns, and then stopped in front of a heavy door. He searched on his key ring, found the right key, fitted it into the lock, and turned it with difficulty. The door swung open to an unusual sight. It would appear that the room had been wallpapered with feathers.

Everyone gasped and Mr. Pym took it for a compliment. "It is rather special, isn't it?" he said. "Yes, rather special. I come in here sometimes and I feel as if I were hiding under a great bird's wing."

"It is like that," said John. "A big bird's wing."

"And we are the little birds," said Mary Abby.

"Yes," said Mr. Pym. "That's the way I feel myself." Then he pointed to one of the walls. "These are glaucous," he said. "I know that. These are Icelandic, I'm pretty sure. This wall is unclassified." And he opened the door to another room which looked just the same. "I'm going to leave this collection to the University," he said. "It will make them the only university with a gull feather collection. I should think they would be overjoyed to receive it, wouldn't you?"

"They should be," said Professor Diggins. "Though it may never have crossed their minds."

"I thought it would be a sort of surprise," said Mr. Pym.

"It will be," said the Professor. "And speaking of the University, tomorrow we shall have to be packing and putting the grove in order. It is time for us to return to Guardian Hill." The children sighed.

"I think," said Mr. Pym, "that if you invite me I shall ride back to Guardian Hill with you. I have an errand to do in town."

"A pleasure," said the Professor. "And now I think we must say our thank yous and good nights."

"But where is Lydia?" asked Jarmes, looking around.

"Where indeed?" said the Professor. And they started to hunt. They found her at last, in the pantry helping Moffitt dry the dishes while Mrs. Moffitt washed up.

"Lydia!" cried Jarmes. "You're *working!*"

"I just somehow seemed to feel like it," said Lydia, a little embarrassed.

CHAPTER XIV

A Surprise for the Professor

The last beans were picked from the vines in the window boxes, the salt water tank carefully covered with the tarpaulin that had once covered the clambake, the pine grove neatly swept, the private rooms regretfully abandoned. John put up a sign that said GONE FOR THE WINTER, and Orson sadly returned his snails to their families among the rocks, never having found anything to significantly excite them, although for a while it looked as though they liked carrots rather a lot. Jarmes packed his bracelets, necklaces, and ashtrays into a large potato sack and it was satisfyingly heavy.

And then Mr. Pym arrived in the grove and they were off and on the way back to Guardian Hill.

There was more quiet than conversation on the way home. There was a great deal to think about. And it was confusing, too, to feel so sorry to leave and yet so full of anticipation. They looked out of the bus windows and watched the seashore disappear and then, gradually, the town grow closer. And all the while Professor Diggins kept up his familiar traveling ditty which seemed to serve him as a road map served others.

As they came through the town and passed the gate of the University, Professor Diggins said, "I shall just stop off here a moment and tell them at the administration office that I am back. I shan't be a moment." And he brought the bus to a stop.

When the Professor had left the bus, Mr. Pym turned to the children and looked at them from under his brows —a bit shyly, as he was still unused to the association of so many people. "I have been racking my brains this whole trip," he said, "and I wonder if I may ask you to help me think."

"What are you trying to think of?" asked Lydia.

"Some kind of a gift for the Professor," said Mr. Pym, blushing a bit. "A kind of remembrance."

"He needs a new celluloid collar," said Mary Abby. "That one is beginning to crack."

Mr. Pym shook his head. "Not quite that sort of thing," he said. And they all started to think.

Then Jarmes picked his head up and said, "He doesn't have a watch on his watch chain, you know."

But Orson said, "Oh, that's because he doesn't really

want one. He says 'Knowing the time isn't what's important; it's knowing what to do with it!' "

"Wait a minute!" John exclaimed suddenly. "I think I
have an idea."

"I'm beginning to get an idea, too," said Orson. Mr.
Pym looked brighter.

"How about this?" asked John. And they all gathered
closer to talk it over . . . whispering, nodding their heads,
and each adding a thought as it occurred.

Meanwhile, Professor Diggins was hurrying up the
long flight of steps that led to the University offices. At
just that moment the Administrator was coming down
the steps and was quite taken aback at the sight of Professor Diggins, in his immaculate black suit and dirty
white sneakers, taking the steps two at a time.

"Ah, there you are, Mr. Administrator," said the Professor, a bit out of breath. "I trust you have been having
a fine summer. I was just coming in to tell you I'm back
and will be in tomorrow to discuss my classes for the new
term. I'll just go and say hello to the Chancellor."

The Administrator cleared his throat nervously and
quickly tried to think of some way to put the Professor

off. The best he could do was to say something not too convincing about how he was quite sure the Chancellor was in conference at the moment.

And just then the Administrator's eyes alighted on the distinctive figure of Mr. Pym who had emerged from the bus and, followed by the children, was making his way up the steps. "My word! exclaimed the Administrator. "Isn't that Mr. Davenport Pym, the trillionaire?"

"Yes," said Professor Diggins as Mr. Pym came to join them. "Mr. Administrator, may I present my friend, Mr. Davenport Pym."

"How do you do, sir," said the Administrator warmly, and for a moment it looked as though he might make a deep bow. "I recognized you from the portrait of your late father. We have his portrait hanging in the library which he so kindly gave the University. You look just like him, just exactly like him. And it would not surprise me if you *were* like him. It wouldn't surprise me at all."

Mr. Pym nodded and scowled. "I wish to speak to the Chancellor," he said.

"Now?" asked the Administrator, looking uncomfortably at Professor Diggins.

"Now," said Mr. Pym. "Why not now?"

"No reason at all, sir," said the Administrator and led the way up the steps. The children, hopping, jumping, and whispering excitedly, joined the procession. As the

Administrator opened the door to the Chancellor's office
a dart flew out of the doorway and struck Mr. Davenport
Pym squarely in the chest.

The Administrator wheeled about and gasped, and
then pulled the dart from Mr. Pym's coat, saying, "It's
just a suction cup, sir, just a suction cup. Don't be
alarmed."

"Oh, do be quiet, if you please!" said Mr. Pym.

The Chancellor was standing aghast, dart held ready for the next shot, and mouth fallen open in horror. Then he gasped, "Mr. Davenport Pym!"

"Ah, the halls of learning!" said Mr. Pym. "How do you do, Chancellor."

"How do you do, Mr. Pym," moaned the Chancellor, extending the dart, and then quickly changing the dart to his left hand and extending his right hand, by which time Mr. Pym had put his hand in his pocket.

"Well," said the Administrator, regaining his composure. "Shall I show Mr. Pym the old gymnasium and the football field, Mr. Chancellor?"

"By all means," said the Chancellor. "By all means. A splendid idea!"

"It's not a splendid idea at all," said Mr. Pym. "I have not the slightest interest in seeing the old gymnasium or the football field. I have come up here for one purpose, to . . ." and he started to search in his coat for something. The children looked over his shoulder and helped him hunt through his pockets, breathing fast with anticipation.

The Professor, meanwhile, was browsing among the books. He picked up several and put them back after leafing through them. And then he picked up *Nomenclature of Pyrotechnics* and upset the housekeeping of the same spider who had had such a hard time the month before in the Administrator's shelves that she had moved into the Chancellor's office.

Mr. Pym had emptied his pockets and laid the contents on the Chancellor's desk. There were some shells, a gull feather, which he smoothed before he laid it down, twenty-seven cents in change, and a crumbled piece of paper. "Ah, here it is," he said, pushing the piece of paper over to the Chancellor.

The Chancellor picked it up, uncrumpled it, and squinted at it. Then he changed his far-away glasses that he used for darts to his near glasses that he used for reading, and holding the piece of paper at arm's length and then pulling it up slowly to his face, he gasped, "A check for one million dollars!"

"Just so," said Mr. Pym.

"Ah," said Professor Diggins, looking up from a book. "That's very nice of you, Mr. Pym. Really, quite nice." The children all chuckled, and Orson stood on one foot, trying not to look bursting with excitement . . . and failed.

The Chancellor was still staring at the check, but the Administrator was pumping Mr. Pym's arm and patting him on the back, until Mr. Pym shook him off like a dog shaking water.

"Ah," said the Chancellor finally, "this is a boon. A really splendid boon. A check for a million dollars! Wait till you see the new gymnasium *that* will build in your name."

Orson put both feet on the ground and stepped forward rather aggressively. Mr. Pym looked coldly at the Chancellor. "If you are planning a new gymnasium in my name, I shall stop the check," he said. "This money has a purpose, and one purpose only." The children all nodded their support.

"And what purpose did you have in mind?" asked the Administrator. "Naturally we shall follow your wishes as to the use of the money."

"Naturally," said Mr. Pym, and he walked over, picked up a rubber dart, and threw it.

"Bull's-eye!" yelled Orson, who was feeling the suspense sorely.

"The purpose of the money," Mr. Pym said, "is to establish a University College of Dragon Hunting, and Professor Diggins here is to be the Dean of the college and its chief lecturer, of course."

"Oh, that's very handsome of you," said Professor Diggins. "What a splendid thing to do! A College of Dragon Hunting!" He seemed for the moment to be quite overwhelmed, and the children came over and hugged his long legs and pulled at his arms.

But the Chancellor's hand with the check was trembling and so was his lower lip. The administrator had

turned a light pink. "D-d-d-dragon hunting!" stammered the Chancellor. "A College of Dragon Hunting!" and he sank into the depths of his leather chair.

"I thought it would surprise you," said Mr. Pym. "And I have another big surprise for you, too. But that's home."

The Administrator rushed over to the Chancellor and started to chafe his hands, speaking in an undertone. "Buck up, sir. A million dollars is a million dollars."

"Well," said Professor Diggins, beginning to recover from the enormous surprise, "this is unquestionably a dream come true. How very kind of you to do this," he said to Mr. Pym. "And how very wise." Mr. Pym looked as though a great warm light were shining on him, and the children were all wearing large Halloween grins.

"Ah, then," said the Professor getting quite serious, "I

shall have to get right to work planning a course of study. Mmmm. Let's see. For the first year we shall try to cover, first, dragon recognition. Yes, I think the first course will be called Recognition. Then, a course in Haunts and Habitats. Then, Methods of Attack, and, of course, Weapons. This will need a lot of planning. I shall be in to discuss the matter with you in the morning, Chancellor. But now I think we should all be getting back to Guardian Hill. Come, everyone!"

The Administrator continued to administer to the Chancellor, who looked entirely dazed. "Buck up, sir," repeated the Administrator. "After all, ha, ha," he laughed, without mirth, "Can't look a gift dragon in the teeth!"

As it had been arranged, Moffitt was waiting in the big old car at the University gate to take Mr. Pym on his errand in town and then drive him back home. They all said good-bye with promises for visits back and forth soon again.

And then the bus was puffing up Guardian Hill. In the late afternoon sun the street blazed a golden welcome to the homecomers, and the group of mothers gathered in front of the Diggins' house was as golden a group of mothers as ever there was—warm and welcoming and marvelous.

"Oh, there's Mama!" cried Lydia. "Look how beautiful she is!"

"She is!" said Jarmes, "she really is!" And he was first out of the bus.

"Orson!" cried Mrs. Peale. "Dear, dear boy! How ever did I manage without you!" Orson graciously allowed himself to be kissed.

Everyone looked at everyone else as though they had

never really seen each other before, and after a suitable amount of hugging and kissing all around, Professor Diggins, having embraced Mrs. Diggins, turned to the group to say good-bye.

"Oh, Professor Diggins," cried Mrs. McGill, "we've been so excited by the children's return we haven't suitably thanked you for the beautiful holiday you've given them."

"No need to, indeed," said Professor Diggins. "They have given me quite as much and more, since there are more of them. Ah, but here's something!" and he raced up the steps of the bus, rummaged about on the baggage rack, and finally came down with a brown paper package which he handed to Mrs. McGill.

"Here are all the socks," he said, "safe and sound."

"Socks?" said Mrs. McGill quizzically, unwrapping the package. "Gracious, they are socks! All colors."

"All the socks, just as you said," said the Professor.

"*I* said?"

"Why, yes. The very last thing you called when we left was 'Remember about their socks!' "

"*I* said that?"

"Absolutely!" The professor turned to bid good-bye to each child, leaving Mrs. McGill still puzzled.

"Jarmes, dear," Mrs. McGill said then, seeing Jarmes

struggling with his heavy potato sack of possessions, "shall I help you carry the rocks?"

"Rocks?" asked Jarmes. "What rocks?"

"Why the beautifully colored beach stones for my garden border . . . the ones I asked you to bring me. Oh, Jarmes, you didn't *forget!* And the *very* last thing I said to you was 'Remember about the rocks.' "

"Oh, *those* rocks," said Jarmes. And then, catching Professor Diggins' eye, he grinned and said, "Some dragon!"

"Well, farewell for now, my young friends," the Professor called.

"Oh dear!" said Lydia. "Is this the end?"

"Indeed not!" said Professor Diggins. "Just a stopping place."

POSSIBILITIES

MUSIC BY

Nanine Elisabeth Valen